ELIZABETH TAYLOR

was born Elizabeth Coles in Reading, Berkshire, in 1912. The daughter of an insurance inspector, she was educated at the Abbey School, Reading, and after leaving school worked as a governess and, later, in a library. At the age of twenty-four she married John William Kendall Taylor, a businessman, with whom she had a son and a daughter.

Elizabeth Taylor wrote her first novel, *At Mrs Lippincote's* (1945), during the war while her husband was in the Royal Air Force. This was followed by *Palladian* (1946), *A View of the Harbour* (1947), *A Wreath of Roses* (1949), *A Game of Hide-and-Seek* (1951), *The Sleeping Beauty* (1953), *Angel* (1957), *In a Summer Season* (1961), *The Soul of Kindness* (1964), *The Wedding Group* (1968), *Mrs Palfrey at the Claremont* (1971) and *Blaming*, published posthumously in 1976. She has also published four volumes of short stories: *Hester Lilly and Other Stories* (1954), *The Blush and Other Stories* (1958), *A Dedicated Man and Other Stories* (1965) and *The Devastating Boys* (1972). Elizabeth Taylor has written a book for children, *Mossy Trotter* (1967); her short stories have been published in the *New Yorker, Harper's Bazaar, Harper's* magazine, *Vogue* and the *Saturday Evening Post*, and she is included in *Penguin Modern Stories 6*.

Elizabeth Taylor lived much of her married life in the village of Penn in Buckinghamshire. She died in 1975.

Critically Elizabeth Taylor is one of the most acclaimed British novelists of this century, and in 1984 *Angel* was selected as one of the Book Marketing Council's "Best Novels of Our Time". Virago publish eight of her sixteen works of fiction.

THE
DEVASTATING
BOYS

AND OTHER STORIES

ELIZABETH TAYLOR

With a New Introduction by
Paul Bailey

PENGUIN BOOKS — VIRAGO PRESS

PENGUIN BOOKS
Viking Penguin Inc., 40 West 23rd Street,
New York, New York 10010, U.S.A.
Penguin Books Ltd, Harmondsworth,
Middlesex, England
Penguin Books Australia Ltd, Ringwood,
Victoria, Australia
Penguin Books Canada Limited, 2801 John Street,
Markham, Ontario, Canada L3R 1B4
Penguin Books (N.Z.) Ltd, 182–190 Wairau Road,
Auckland 10, New Zealand

First published in Great Britain by Chatto & Windus Ltd. 1972
First published in the United States of America by
Viking Penguin Inc. 1972
This edition first published in Great Britain by
Virago Press Limited 1984
Published in Penguin Books 1985

ISBN 0 14 016.106 6

Printed in the United States of America by
R. R. Donnelley & Sons Company
Harrisonburg, Virginia

Acknowledgements

The Author would like to thank the Editors of the following publications in which these stories first appeared: *Saturday Evening Post*; *Homes and Gardens*; *McCall's*; *The Cornhill*; *The New Yorker*; *Penguin Modern Stories*; *London Magazine*.

To
HARRIET, MATTHEW, REBECCA
and
FLORA

Contents

Introduction

"She seemed to have been made for widowhood, and had her own little set, for bridge and coffee mornings, and her committee-meetings for the better known charities—such as the National Society for the Prevention of Cruelty to Children, and the Royal Society for the Prevention of Cruelty to Animals."

Elizabeth Taylor is describing, with her customary economy, the complacent Mrs Mason in the story "Sisters". "Made for widowhood", "better known charities"—with such slyly placed phrases, she puts a whole life into focus. "She had no money worries, no worries of any kind. Childless and serene, she lived from day to day . . ." the storyteller continues, adding details to the portrait by subtle degrees:

> After tea, her friends' husbands came home, and then Mrs Mason pottered in her garden, played patience in the winter, or read historical romances from the library. "Something light," she would tell the assistant, as if seeking suggestions from a waiter. She could never remember the names of authors or their works, and it was quite a little disappointment when she discovered that she had read a novel before. She had few other disappointments—nothing much more than an unexpected shower of rain, or a tough cutlet, or a girl at the hairdresser's getting her rinse wrong.

Mrs Mason is the perfect subject for a short story. This respected figure in an English county town, a "regular" at the Oak Beams Tea Room, is too slight a woman (in terms of character, that is) to be analysed or inspected at length. Someone who curls up with Cartland or Jean Plaidy and experiences "quite a little disappointment" if she has encountered their swashbucklers, villains and hoity-toity heroines before, hardly merits the attention afforded an Emma Woodhouse, say, or a Gwendolen Harleth. Mrs Mason's pitiable rectitude would soon become tiresome after a couple of chapters.

As it is, within the confines of "Sisters"—a mere ten pages or so—this trivial human being, with her extremely conventional notions of what is respectable and what isn't, is brought to the necessarily brief fictional life that she merits by a writer who thrived on the possibilities of brevity. The short-story form is one that attracts the swift glance rather than the long, cold stare, and Elizabeth Taylor is one of the great glancers. Her detractors, among whom Anthony Burgess is by far the most vociferous, won't allow her her miniaturist's distinction—but then, he and they are on a constant quest for size, scope, relevance and Importance. Elizabeth Taylor couldn't be bothered to be important. She knew her limitations and worked within them accordingly. She opted for accuracy, honesty, and a controlled delight in exposing human folly as it is practised in polite society in the neat and tidy Home Counties.

The ever-global Burgess reserves for her the ultimate insult: her writing is too *English*. *English* stands for parochialism, provincialism, things of minor significance. If you actually read Elizabeth

Taylor properly, you become aware that her insights
into parochialism, etc., are extraordinarily percep-
tive—those swift glances don't miss a single
self-deceiving trick. And if the English provinces
exist, why should they be denied such a shrewd
recorder, especially one who records with such grace
and wit? This *English* sneer has outstayed its
welcome: novelists who limit their interests to Jewish
intellectual life in New York City are not held in
contempt for being *American*. Some of the very worst
living authors are *International*.

That diatribe over, let me say that *The Devastating
Boys* is a collection that still delights me, after several
readings. The title story, for example, is an absolute
stunner: two ways of contemporary English life are
brought together to make a little work of art that is as
funny as it is touching. The boys themselves, the
half-caste Benny and the West-Indian Septimus, are
beautifully realised ("Benny had a mock-suède coat
with a nylon-fur collar and a trilby hat with a
feather") without a hint of condescension. Their
London talk is perfectly caught, with no recourse to
dropped aitches and the other short-cuts employed
by the tin-eared when they are dealing with the
proletariat in their fiction. Elizabeth Taylor has
delicious fun with the boys' gift for mimicry. She has
them, in fact, mimicking the affected speech of a
rather bad novelist—bad by implication, for she has
no need to spell out the nature of that badness.

Another gem here is "Flesh", in which a publican's
blowsy wife, Phyl, who has recently had a

hysterectomy has an enchanted meeting with the newly bereaved Stanley in one of those ghastly Mediterranean seaside resorts from which the natives are wisely absent. Phyl and Stanley decide to have a fling, and it is what happens when that fling actually takes place that is the concern of the story. Phyl's blowsiness, her use of ancient saloon-bar catch-phrases, her taste for "loud" clothes, are never satirised, as they so easily could have been. As a consequence, "Flesh" maintains a balance between the hilarious and the poignant. Phyl's and Stanley's embarrassments are humanely accounted for, not set up for abusive laughter.

"The Fly-Paper" is the odd one out among these eleven stories, if only because it deals with the macabre. The tone is, once again, perfectly caught and sustained—the drably ordinary gradually and almost imperceptibly changing into the menacing. Horrors of the Stephen King kind are a world away from the one Elizabeth Taylor glances at in this little tale of an unhappy girl's chance meeting on a country bus. What happens at the close of 'The Fly-Paper' is genuinely and believably horrific, not concocted for spine-chilling effect—it's the stuff of a thousand desolating newspaper reports.

I could go on extolling the virtues of each story in *The Devastating Boys*, but I shall refrain from doing so, in order not to lessen the pleasure that awaits new readers. What I shall commend is the sheer freshness of the writing throughout the book. There are no flourishes or obvious conceits in this prose, just clarity, exactness of glancing eye and craftily poised ear, and an undemonstrative humanity. The art of the miniaturist, English variety, is displayed at its best in "Miss A. and Miss M.", in "Hôtel Du Commerce", with its surprising but credible ending, in the deeply sad "Tall Boy"—oh, in every single, incomparable one of them. Burgess and his bully-boys of Lit. Crit., praising the obscure and the loftily near-literate, can go on belittling her, but she will survive. Elizabeth Taylor wanted to be a painter, and it's of a painter I always think when I consider her artistry—Gwen John, whose modest greatness is at last being recognised. You can love Titian and still love Gwen John. You can love George Eliot, as I do, and still love what Elizabeth Taylor achieved, as I do, intensely.

Paul Bailey
London, 1984

The Devastating Boys

LAURA was always too early; and this was as bad as being late, her husband, who was always late himself, told her. She sat in her car in the empty railway-station approach, feeling very sick, from dread.

It was half-past eleven on a summer morning. The country station was almost spellbound in silence, and there was, to Laura, a dreadful sense of self-absorption—in herself—in the stillness of the only porter standing on the platform, staring down the line: even—perhaps especially—in inanimate things; all were menacingly intent on being themselves, and separately themselves—the slanting shadow of railings across the platform, the glossiness of leaves, and the closed door of the office looking more closed, she thought, than any door she had ever seen.

She got out of the car and went into the station walking up and down the platform in a panic. It was a beautiful morning. If only the children weren't coming then she could have enjoyed it.

The children were coming from London. It was Harold's idea to have them, some time back, in March, when he read of a scheme to give London children a summer holiday in the country. This he might have read without interest, but the words "Some of the children will be coloured" caught his eye. He seemed to find a slight tinge of warning in the phrase; the more he thought it over, the more he was convinced. He had made a long speech to Laura about children being the great equalisers, and that we should learn from them, that to insinuate the stale prejudices of their elders into their fresh, fair minds was such a sin that he could not think of a worse one.

He knew very little about children. His students had passed beyond the blessed age, and shades of the prison-house had closed about them. His own children were even older, grown-up and gone away; but, while they were young, they had done nothing to destroy his faith in them, or blur the idea of them he had in his mind, and his feeling of humility in their presence. They had been good children carefully dealt with and easy to handle. There had scarcely been a cloud over their growing-up. Any little bothers Laura had hidden from him.

In March, the end of July was a long way away. Laura, who was lonely in middle-age, seemed to herself to be frittering away her days, just waiting for her grandchildren to be born: she had agreed with Harold's suggestion. She would have agreed anyway, whatever it was, as it was her nature—and his—for her to do so. It would be rather exciting to have two children to stay—to have the beds in Imogen's and Lalage's room slept in again. "We could have two boys, or two girls," Harold said. "No stipulation, but that they must be coloured."

Now *he* was making differences, but Laura did not remark upon it. All she said was, "What will they do all the time?"

"What our own children used to do—play in the garden, go for picnics . . ."

"On wet days?"

"Dress up," he said at once.

She remembered Imogen and Lalage in her old hats and

dresses, slopping about in her big shoes, see-sawing on high heels, and she had to turn her head away, and there were tears in her eyes.

Her children had been her life, and her grandchildren one day would be; but here was an empty space. Life had fallen away from her. She had never been clever like the other professors' wives, or managed to have what they called 'outside interests'. Committees frightened her, and good works made her feel embarrassed and clumsy.

She *was* a clumsy person—gentle, but clumsy. Pacing up and down the platform, she had an ungainly walk—legs stiffly apart, head a little poked forward because she had poor sight. She was short and squarely-built and her clothes were never right; often she looked dishevelled, sometimes even battered.

This morning, she wore a label pinned to her breast, so that the children's escort would recognise her when the train drew in; but she felt self-conscious about it and covered it with her hand, though there was no one but the porter to see.

The signal dropped, as if a guillotine had come crashing down, and her heart seemed to crash down with it. Two boys! she thought. Somehow, she had imagined girls. She was used to girls, and shy of boys.

The printed form had come a day or two ago and had increased the panic which had gradually been gathering. Six-year-old boys, and she had pictured perhaps eight or ten-year-old girls, whom she could teach to sew and make cakes for tea, and press wild-flowers as she had taught Imogen and Lalage to do.

Flurried and anxious entertaining at home; interviewing

headmistresses; once—shied away from failure—opening a sale-of-work in the village—these agonies to her diffident nature seemed nothing to the nervousness she felt now, as the train appeared round the bend. She simply wasn't good with children—only with her own. *Their* friends had frightened her, had been mouse-quiet and glum, or had got out of hand, and she herself had been too shy either to intrude or clamp down. When she met children—perhaps the small grandchildren of her acquaintances, she would only smile, perhaps awkwardly touch a cheek with her finger. If she were asked to hold a baby, she was fearful lest it should cry, and often it would, sensing lack of assurance in her clasp.

The train came in and slowed up. Suppose that I can't find them, she thought, and she went anxiously from window to window, her label uncovered now. And suppose they cry for their mothers and want to go home.

A tall, authoritative woman, also wearing a label, leaned out of a window, saw her and signalled curtly. She had a compartment full of little children in her charge to be delivered about Oxfordshire. Only two got out onto this platform, Laura's two, Septimus Smith and Benny Reece. They wore tickets, too, with their names printed on them.

Benny was much lighter in complexion than Septimus. He was obviously a half-caste and Laura hoped that this would count in Harold's eyes. It might even be one point up. They stood on the platform, looking about them, holding their little cardboard cases.

"My name is Laura," she said. She stooped and clasped them to her in terror, and kissed their cheeks. Sep's in particular, was extraordinarily soft, like the petal of a poppy. His big eyes stared up at her, without expression. He wore a dark, long-trousered suit, so that he was all over sombre and unchildlike. Benny had a mock-suède coat with a nylon-fur collar and a trilby hat with a feather. They did not speak. Not only was she, Laura, strange to them, but they were strange to one another. There had only been a short train-journey in which to sum up their chances of becoming friends.

She put them both into the back of the car, so that there should be no favouritism, and drove off, pointing out— to utter silence—places on the way. "That's a café where we'll go for tea one day." The silence was dreadful. "A caff," she amended. "And there's the little cinema. Not very grand, I'm afraid. Not like London ones."

They did not even glance about them.

"Are you going to be good friends to one another?" she asked.

After a pause, Sep said in a slow grave voice, "Yeah, I'm going to be a good friend."

"Is this the country?" Benny asked. He had a chirpy, perky Cockney voice and accent.

"Yeah, this is the countryside," said Sep, in his rolling drawl, glancing indifferently at some trees.

Then he began to talk. It was in an aggrieved sing-song. "I don't go on that train no more. I don't like that train, and I don't go on that again over my dead body. Some boy he say to me, 'You don't sit in that corner seat. I sit there.' I say, 'You don't sit here. I sit here.' 'Yeah,' I say, 'You don't own this train, so I don't budge from here.' Then he dash my comic down and tore it."

"Yep, he tore his comic," Benny said.

" 'You tear my comic, you buy me another comic,' I said. 'Or else.' 'Or *else*,' I said." He suddenly broke off and looked at a wood they were passing. "I don't go near those tall bushes. They full of snakes what sting you."

"No, they ain't," said Benny.

"My Mam said so. I don't go."

"There aren't any snakes," said Laura, in a light voice. She, too, had a terror of them, and was afraid to walk through bracken. "Or only little harmless ones," she added.

"I don't go," Sep murmured to himself. Then, in a louder voice, he went on. "He said, 'I don't buy no comic for you, you nigger,' he said."

"He never said that," Benny protested.

"Yes, 'You dirty nigger,' he said."

"He never."

There was something so puzzled in Benny's voice that Laura immediately believed him. The expression on his little monkey-face was open and impartial.

"I don't go on that train no more."

"You've got to. When you go home," Benny said.

"Maybe I don't go home."

"We'll think about that later. You've only just arrived," said Laura, smiling.

"No, I think about that right now."

Along the narrow lane to the house, they were held up by the cows from the farm. A boy drove them along, whacking their messed rumps with a stick. Cow-pats plopped onto the road and steamed there, zizzing with flies. Benny held his nose and Sep, glancing at him, at once did the same. "I don't care for this smell of the country-side," he complained in a pinched tone.

"No, the countryside stinks," said Benny.

"Cows frighten me."

"They don't frighten me."

Sep cringed against the back of the seat, whimpering; but Benny wound his window right down, put his head a little out of it, and shouted, "Get on, you dirty old sods, or else I'll show you."

"Hush," said Laura gently.

"He swore," Sep pointed out.

They turned into Laura's gateway, up the short drive. In front of the house was a lawn and a cedar tree. From one of its lower branches hung the old swing, on chains, waiting for Laura's grandchildren.

The boys clambered out of the car and followed her into the hall, where they stood looking about them criti-cally; then Benny dropped his case and shot like an arrow towards Harold's golf-bag and pulled out a club. His face was suddenly bright with excitement and Laura, darting forward to him, felt a stab of misery at having to begin the 'No's' so soon. "I'm afraid Harold wouldn't like you to touch them," she said. Benny stared her out, but after a moment or two gave up the club with all the unwilling-ness in the world. Meanwhile, Sep had taken an antique coaching-horn and was blowing a bubbly, uneven blast on it, his eyes stretched wide and his cheeks blown out. "Nor that," said Laura faintly, taking it away. "Let's go upstairs and unpack."

They appeared not at all overawed by the size of this fairly large house; in fact, rather unimpressed by it.

In the room where once, as little girls, Imogen and Lalage had slept together, they opened their cases. Sep put his clothes neatly and carefully into his drawer; and Benny tipped the case into his—comics, clothes and shoes, and a scattering of peanuts. I'll tidy it later, Laura thought.

"Shall we toss up for who sleeps by the window?" she suggested.

"I don't sleep by no window," said Sep. "I sleep in *this* bed; with *him*."

"I want to sleep by myself," said Benny.

Sep began a babyish whimpering, which increased into an anguished keening. "I don't like to sleep in the bed by myself. I'm scared to. I'm real scared to. I'm scared."

This was entirely theatrical, Laura decided, and Benny seemed to think so, too; for he took no notice.

A fortnight! Laura thought. This day alone stretched endlessly before her, and she dared not think of any following ones. Already she felt ineffectual and had an inkling that they were going to despise her. And her brightness was false and not infectious. She longed for Harold to come home, as she had never longed before.

"I reckon I go and clean my teeth," said Sep, who had broken off his dirge.

"Lunch is ready. Afterwards would be more sensible, surely?" Laura suggested.

But they paid no heed to her. Both took their toothbrushes, their new tubes of paste, and rushed to find the bathroom. "I'm going to bathe myself," said Sep. "I'm going to bathe all my skin, and wash my head."

"Not *before* lunch," Laura called out, hastening after them; but they did not hear her. Taps were running and steam clouding the window, and Sep was tearing off his clothes.

"He's bathed three times already," Laura told Harold. She had just come downstairs, and had done so as soon as she heard him slamming the front door.

Upstairs, Sep was sitting in the bath. She had made him a lacy vest of soap-froth, as once she had made them for Imogen and Lalage. It showed up much better on his grape-dark skin. He sat there, like a tribal warrior done up in war-paint.

Benny would not go near the bath. He washed at the basin, his sleeves rolled up: and he turned the cake of soap over and over uncertainly in his hands.

"It's probably a novelty," Harold said, referring to Sep's bathing. "Would you like a drink?"

"Later perhaps. I daren't sit down, for I'd never get up again."

"I'll finish them off. I'll go and see to them. You just sit there and drink this."

"Oh, Harold, how wonderfully good of you."

She sank down on the arm of a chair, and sipped her drink, feeling stunned. From the echoing bathroom came shouts of laughter, and it was very good to hear them, especially from a distance. Harold was being a great success, and relief and gratitude filled her.

After a little rest, she got up and went weakly about the room, putting things back in their places. When this was done, the room still looked wrong. An unfamiliar dust seemed to have settled all over it, yet, running a finger over the piano, she found none. All the same, it was not the usual scene she set for Harold's home-coming in the evenings. It had taken a shaking-up.

Scampering footsteps now thundered along the landing. She waited a moment or two, then went upstairs. They were in bed, in separate beds; Benny by the window. Harold was pacing about the room, telling them a story: his hands flapped like huge ears at either side of his face; then he made an elephant's trunk with his arm. From the beds, the children's eyes stared unblinkingly at him. As Laura came into the room, only Benny's flickered in her direction, then back at once to the magic of Harold's performance. She blew a vague, unheeded kiss, and crept away.

"It's like seeing snow begin to fall," Harold said at dinner. "You know it's going to be a damned nuisance, but it makes a change."

He sounded exhilarated; clashed the knife against the steel with vigour, and started to carve. He kept popping little titbits into his mouth. Carver's perks, he called them.

"Not much for me," Laura said.

"What did they have for lunch?"

"Fish-cakes."

"Enjoy them?"

"Sep said, 'I don't like that.' He's very suspicious, and that makes Benny all the braver. Then he eats too much, showing off."

"They'll settle down," Harold said, settling down himself to his dinner. After a while, he said, "The little

18

Cockney one asked me just now if this were a private house. When I said 'Yes', he said, 'I thought it was, because you've got the sleeping upstairs and the talking downstairs.' Didn't quite get the drift."

"Pathetic," Laura murmured.

"I suppose where they come from, it's all done in the same room."

"Yes, it is."

"Pathetic," Harold said in his turn.

"It makes me feel ashamed."

"Oh, come now."

"And wonder if we're doing the right thing—perhaps unsettling them for what they have to go back to."

"My dear girl," he said. "Damn it, those people who organise these things know what they're doing."

"I suppose so."

"They've been doing it for years."

"Yes, I know."

"Well, then . . ."

Suddenly she put down her knife and fork and rested her forehead in her hands.

"What's up, old thing?" Harold asked, with his mouth full.

"Only tired."

"Well, they've dropped off all right. You can have a quiet evening."

"I'm too tired to sit up straight any longer." After a silence, lifting her face from her hands, she said, "Thirteen more days! What shall I do with them all that time?"

"Take them for scrambles in the woods," he began, sure that he had endless ideas.

"I tried. They won't walk a step. They both groaned and moaned so much that we turned back."

"Well, they can play on the swing."

"For how long, how *long*? They soon got tired of that. Anyhow, they quarrel about one having a longer turn than the other. In the end, I gave them the egg-timer."

"That was a good idea."

"They broke it."

"Oh."

"Please God, don't let it rain," she said earnestly, staring out of the window. "Not for the next fortnight, anyway."

The next day, it rained from early morning. After breakfast, when Harold had gone off, Laura settled the boys at the dining-room table with a snakes-and-ladders board. As they had never played it, she had to draw up a chair herself, and join in. By some freakish chance, Benny threw one six after another, would, it seemed, never stop; and Sep's frustration and fury rose. He kept snatching the dice-cup away from Benny, peering into it, convinced of trickery. The game went badly for him and Laura, counting rapidly ahead, saw that he was due for the longest snake of all. His face was agonised, his dark hand, with its pale scars and scratches, hovered above the board; but he could not bring himself to draw the counter down the snake's horrid speckled length.

"I'll do it for you," Laura said. He shuddered, and turned aside. Then he pushed his chair back from the table and lay, face-down on the floor, silent with grief.

"And it's not yet ten o'clock," thought Laura, and was relieved to see Mrs Milner, the help, coming up the path under her umbrella. It was a mercy that it was her morning.

She finished off the game with Benny, and he won; but the true glory of victory had been taken from him by the vanquished, lying still and wounded on the hearth-rug. Laura was bright and cheerful about being beaten, trying to set an example; but she made no impression.

Presently, in exasperation, she asked, "Don't you play games at school?"

There was no answer for a time, then Benny, knowing the question wasn't addressed to him, said, "Yep, sometimes."

"And what do you do if you lose?" Laura asked, glancing down at the hearth-rug. "You can't win all the time."

In a muffled voice, Sep at last said, "I don't win *any* time. They won't let me win any time."

"It's only luck."

"No, they don't *let* me win. I just go and lie down and shut my eyes."

"And are these our young visitors?" asked Mrs Milner, coming in with the vacuum-cleaner. Benny stared at her; Sep lifted his head from his sleeve for a brief look, and then returned to his sulking.

"What a nasty morning I've brought with me," Mrs Milner said, after Laura had introduced them.

"You brought a nasty old morning all right," Sep agreed, mumbling into his jersey.

"But," she went on brightly, putting her hands into her overall pockets. "I've also brought some lollies."

Benny straightened his back in anticipation. Sep, peeping with one eye, stretched out an arm.

"That's if Madam says you may."

"They call me 'Laura'." It had been Harold's idea and Laura had foreseen this very difficulty.

Mrs Milner could not bring herself to say the name and she, too, could foresee awkwardnesses.

"No, Sep," said Laura firmly. "Either you get up properly and take it politely, or you go without."

She wished that Benny hadn't at once scrambled to his feet and stood there at attention. Sep buried his head again and moaned. All the sufferings of his race were upon him at this moment.

Benny took his sweet and made a great appreciative fuss about it.

All the china had gone up a shelf or two, out of reach, Mrs Milner noted. It was like the old days, when Imogen's and Lalage's friends had come to tea.

"Now, there's a good lad," she said, stepping over Sep, and plugging in the vacuum-cleaner.

"Is that your sister?" Benny asked Laura, when Mrs Milner had brought in the pudding, gone out again, and closed the door.

"No, Mrs Milner comes to help me with the housework —every Tuesday and Friday."

"She must be a very kind old lady," Benny said.

"Do you like that?" Laura asked Sep, who was pushing jelly into his spoon with his fingers.

"Yeah, I like this fine."

He had suddenly cheered up. He did not mention the lolly, which Mrs Milner had put back in her pocket. All the rest of the morning, they had played excitedly with the telephone—one upstairs, in Laura's bedroom; the other downstairs, in the hall—chattering and shouting to one another, and running to Laura to come to listen.

That evening, Harold was home earlier than usual and could not wait to complain that he had tried all day to telephone.

"I know, dear," Laura said. "I should have stopped them, but it gave me a rest."

"You'll be making a rod for everybody's back, if you let them do just what they like all the time."

"It's for such a short while—well, relatively speaking— and they haven't got telephones at home, so the question doesn't arise."

"But other people might want to ring you up."

"So few ever do, it's not worth considering."

"Well, someone did today. Helena Western."

"What on earth for?"

"There's no need to look frightened. She wants you to take the boys to tea." Saying this, his voice was full of satisfaction, for he admired Helena's husband. Helena herself wrote what he referred to as 'clever-clever little novels'. He went on sarcastically, "She saw you with them from the top of a bus, and asked me when I met her later in Blackwell's. She says she has absolutely *no* feelings about coloured people, as some of her friends apparently have." He was speaking in Helena's way of stresses and breathings. "In fact," he ended, "she rather goes out of her way to be extra pleasant to them."

"So she does have feelings," Laura said.

She was terrified at the idea of taking the children to tea with Helena. She always felt dull and overawed in her company, and was afraid that the boys would misbehave and get out of her control, and then Helena would put it all into a novel. Already she had put Harold in one; but, luckily, he had not recognised his own transformation from professor of archaeology to barrister. Her simple trick worked, as far as he was concerned. To Harold, that character, with his vaguely left-wing opinions and opinionated turns of phrase, his quelling manner to his wife, his very appearance, could have nothing to do with him, since he had never taken silk. Everyone else had recognised and known, and Laura, among them, knew they had.

"I'll ring her up," she said; but she didn't stir from her chair, sat staring wearily in front of her, her hands on her knees—a very resigned old woman's attitude; Whistler's mother. "I'm *too* old," she thought. "I'd be too old for my own grandchildren." But she had never imagined *them* like the ones upstairs in bed. She had pictured biddable little children, like Lalage and Imogen.

"They're good at *night*," she said to Harold, continuing her thoughts aloud. "They lie there and talk quietly, *once* they're in bed. I wonder what they talk about. Us, perhaps." It was an alarming idea.

In the night she woke and remembered that she had not telephoned Helena. "I'll do it after breakfast," she thought.

But she was still making toast when the telephone rang,

and the boys left the table and raced to the hall ahead of her. Benny was first and, as he grabbed the receiver, Sep stood close by him, ready to shout some messages into the magical instrument. Laura hovered anxiously by, but Benny warned her off with staring eyes. "Be polite," she whispered imploringly.

"Yep, my name's Benny," he was saying.

Then he listened, with a look of rapture. It was his first real telephone conversation, and Sep was standing by, shivering with impatience and envy.

"Yep, that'll be O.K.," said Benny, grinning. "What day?"

Laura put out her hand, but he shrank back, clutching the receiver. "I got the message," he hissed at her. "Yep, he's here," he said, into the telephone. Sep smiled self-consciously and drew himself up as he took the receiver. "Yeah, I am Septimus Alexander Smith." He gave his high, bubbly chuckle. "Sure I'll come there." To prolong the conversation, he went on, "Can my friend, Benny Reece come, too? Can Laura come?" Then he frowned, looking up at the ceiling, as if for inspiration. "Can my father, Alexander Leroy Smith come?"

Laura made another darting movement.

"Well, no, he can't then," Sep said, "because he's dead."

This doubled him up with mirth, and it was a long time before he could bring himself to say goodbye. When he had done so, he quickly put the receiver down.

"Someone asked me to tea," he told Laura. "I said, 'Yeah, sure I come.'"

"And me," said Benny.

"Who was it?" Laura asked, although she knew.

"I don't know," said Sep. "I don't know *who* that was."

When later and secretly, Laura telephoned Helena, Helena said, "Aren't they simply *devastating* boys?"

"How did the tea-party go?" Harold asked.

They had all arrived back home together—he, from a meeting; Laura and the boys from Helena's.

"They were good," Laura said, which was all that mattered. She drew them to her, one on either side. It was her movement of gratitude towards them. They had not let her down. They had played quietly at a fishing game with real water and magnetised tin fish, had eaten unfamiliar things, such as anchovy toast and brandy-snaps without any expression of alarm or revulsion: they had helped carry the tea things indoors from the lawn. Helena had been surprisingly clever with them. She made them laugh, as seldom Laura could. She struck the right note from the beginning. When Benny picked up sixpence from the gravelled path, she thanked him casually and put it in her pocket. Laura was grateful to her for that and proud that Benny ran away at once so unconcernedly. When Helena had praised them for their good behaviour, Laura had blushed with pleasure, just as if they were her own children.

"She is really very nice," Laura said later, thinking still of her successful afternoon with Helena.

"Yes, she talks too much, that's all."

Harold was pleased with Laura for having got on well with his colleague's wife. It was so long since he had tried to urge Laura into academic circles, and for years he had given up trying. Now, sensing his pleasure, her own was enhanced.

"When we were coming away," Laura said, "Helena whispered to me, 'Aren't they simply *dev*astating?' "

"You've exactly caught her tone."

At that moment, they heard from the garden, Benny also exactly catching her tone.

"Let's have the bat, there's a little pet," he mimicked, trying to snatch the old tennis-racquet from Sep.

"You sod off," drawled Sep.

"Oh, my dear, you shake me rigid."

Sep began his doubling-up-with-laughter routine; first, in silence, bowed over, lifting one leg then another up to his chest, stamping the ground. It was like the start of a tribal dance, Laura thought, watching him from the window; then the pace quickened, he skipped about, and laughed, with his head thrown back, and tears rolled down his face. Benny looked on, smirking a little, obviously proud that his wit should have had such an effect. Round and round went Sep, his loose limbs moving like pistons. "Yeah, you shake me rigid," he shouted. "You shake me entirely rigid." Benny, after hesitating, joined in. They circled the lawn, and disappeared into the shrubbery.

"She *did* say that. Helena," Laura said, turning to Harold. "When Benny was going on about something he'd done she said, 'My dear, you shake me entirely rigid.' " Then Laura added thoughtfully, "I wonder if they are as good at imitating *us*, when they're lying up there in bed, talking."

"A sobering thought," said Harold, who could not believe he had any particular idiosyncrasies to be copied. "Oh, God, someone's broken one of my sherds," he suddenly cried, stooping to pick up two pieces of pottery from the floor. His agonised shout brought Sep to the french windows, and he stood there, bewildered.

As the pottery had been broken before, he hadn't bothered to pick it up, or confess. The day before, he had broken a whole cup and nothing had happened. Now this grown man was bowed over as if in pain, staring at the fragments in his hand. Sep crept back into the shrubbery.

The fortnight, miraculously, was passing. Laura could now say, "This time next week." She would do gardening, get her hair done, clean all the paint. Often, she wondered about the kind of homes the other children had gone to—those children she had glimpsed on the train; and she imagined them staying on farms, helping with the animals, looked after by buxom farmers'-wives—pale London children, growing gratifyingly brown, filling out, going home at last with roses in their cheeks. She could see no difference in Sep and Benny.

What they had really got from the holiday was one another. It touched her to see them going off into the shrubbery with arms about one another's shoulders, and to listen to their peaceful murmuring as they lay in bed, to hear their shared jokes. They quarrelled a great deal, over the tennis-racquet or Harold's old cricket-bat, and Sep was constantly casting himself down on the grass and weeping, if he were out at cricket, or could not get Benny out.

It was he who would sit for hours with his eyes fixed on Laura's face while she read to him. Benny would wander restlessly about, waiting for the story to be finished. If he interrupted, Sep would put his hand imploringly on Laura's arm, silently willing her to continue.

Benny liked her to play the piano. It was the only time she was admired. They would dance gravely about the room, with their bottles of Coca-Cola, sucking through straws, choking, heads bobbing up and down. Once, at the end of a concert of nursery-rhymes, Laura played *God Save the Queen*, and Sep rushed at her, trying to shut the lid down on her hands. "I don't like that," he keened. "My Mam don't like *God Save the Queen* neither. She say 'God save *me*'."

"Get out," said Benny, kicking him on the shin. "You're shaking me entirely rigid."

On the second Sunday, they decided that they must go to church. They had a sudden curiosity about it, and a yearning to sing hymns.

"Well, take them," said liberal-minded and agnostic Harold to Laura.

But it was almost time to put the sirloin into the oven. "We did sign that form," she said in a low voice. "To say we'd take them if they wanted to go."

"Do you *really* want to go?" Harold asked, turning to the boys, who were wanting to go more and more as the discussion went on. "Oh, God!" he groaned—inappropriately, Laura thought.

"What religion are you, anyway?" he asked them.

"I am a Christian," Sep said with great dignity.

"Me, too," said Benny.

"What time does it begin?" Harold asked, turning his back to Laura.

"At eleven o'clock."

"Isn't there some kids' service they can go to on their own?"

"Not in August, I'm afraid."

"Oh, God!" he said again.

Laura watched them setting out; rather overawed, the two boys; it was the first time they had been out alone with him.

She had a quiet morning in the kitchen. Not long after twelve o'clock they returned. The boys at once raced for the cricket-bat, and fought over it, while Harold poured himself out a glass of beer.

"How did it go?" asked Laura.

"Awful! Lord, I felt such a fool."

"Did they misbehave, then?"

"Oh, no, they were perfectly good—except that for some reason Benny kept holding his nose. But I knew so many people there. And the Vicar shook hands with me afterwards and said, 'We are especially glad to see *you*.' The embarrassment!"

"It must have shaken you entirely rigid," Laura said, smiling as she basted the beef. Harold looked at her as if for the first time in years. She so seldom tried to be amusing.

At lunch, she asked the boys if they had enjoyed their morning.

"Church smelt nasty," Benny said, making a face.

"Yeah," agreed Sep. "I prefer my own country. I prefer Christians."

"Me, too," Benny said. "Give me Christians any day."

"Has it been a success?" Laura asked Harold. "For them, I mean."

It was their last night—Sep's and Benny's—and she wondered if her feeling of being on the verge of tears was entirely from tiredness. For the past fortnight, she had reeled into bed, and slept without moving.

A success for *them?* She could not be quite sure; but it had been a success for her, and for Harold. In the evenings, they had so much to talk about, and Harold, basking in his popularity, had been genial and considerate.

Laura, the boys had treated as a piece of furniture, or a slave, and humbly she accepted her place in their minds. She was a woman who had never had any high opinions of herself.

"No more cricket," she said. She had been made to play for hours—always wicket-keeper, running into the shrubs for lost balls while Sep and Benny rested full-length on the grass.

"He has a lovely action," she had said to Harold one evening, watching Sep taking his long run up to bowl. "He might be a great athlete one day."

"It couldn't happen," Harold said. "Don't you see, he has rickets?"

One of her children with rickets, she had thought, stricken.

Now, on this last evening, the children were in bed. She and Harold were sitting by the drawing-room window, talking about them. There was a sudden scampering along the landing and Laura said, "It's only one of them going to the toilet."

"The *what?*"

"They ticked me off for saying 'lavatory'," she said placidly. "Benny said it was a bad word."

She loved to make Harold laugh, and several times lately she had managed to amuse him, with stories she had to recount.

"I shan't like saying goodbye," she said awkwardly.

"No," said Harold. He got up and walked about the room, examined his shelves of pottery fragments. "It's been a lot of work for you, Laura."

She looked away shyly. There had been almost a note of praise in his voice. "Tomorrow," she thought. "I hope I don't cry."

At the station, it was Benny who cried. All the morning he had talked about his mother, how she would be waiting for him at Paddington station. Laura kept their thoughts fixed on the near future.

Now they sat on a bench on the sunny platform, wearing their name-labels, holding bunches of wilting flowers, and Laura looked at her watch and wished the minutes away. As usual, she was too early. Then she saw Benny shut his eyes quickly, but not in time to stop two tears falling. She was surprised and dismayed. She began to talk brightly, but neither replied. Benny kept his head down, and Sep stared ahead. At last, to her relief, the signal fell, and soon the train came in. She handed them over to the escort, and they sat down in the compartment without a word. Benny gazed out of the further window, away from her, rebukingly; and Sep's face was expressionless.

As the train began to pull out, she stood waving and smiling; but they would not glance in her direction, though the escort was urging them to do so, and setting an example. When at last Laura moved away, her head and throat were aching, and she had such a sense of failure and fatigue that she hardly knew how to walk back to the car.

It was not Mrs Milner's morning, and the house was deadly quiet. Life, noise, laughter, bitter quarrelling had gone out of it. She picked up the cricket-bat from the lawn and went inside. She walked about, listlessly tidying things, putting them back in their places. Then fetched a damp cloth and sat down at the piano and wiped the sticky, dirty keys.

She was sitting there, staring in front of her, clasping the cloth in her lap, when Harold came in.

"I'm taking the afternoon off," he said. "Let's drive out to Minster Lovell for lunch."

She looked at him in astonishment. On his way across the room to fetch his tobacco pouch, he let his hand rest on her shoulder for a moment.

"Don't fret," he said. "I think we've got them for life now."

"Benny cried."

"Extraordinary thing. Shall we make tracks?"

She stood up and closed the lid of the keyboard. "It was awfully nice of you to come back, Harold." She paused, thinking she might say more; but he was puffing away, lighting his pipe with a great fuss, as if he were not listening. "Well, I'll go and get ready," she said.

33

The Excursion to the Source

"ENGLAND was like this when I was a child," Gwenda said. She was fifteen years older than Polly, and had had a brief, baby's glimpse of the gay twenties—though, as an infant, could hardly have been really conscious of their charms.

It was France—the middle of France—which so much resembled that unspoilt England. In the hedgerows grew all the wild-flowers that urbanisation, ribbon-development and sprayed insecticides had turned into rarities, delights of the past, in the South of England where Gwenda and Polly lived.

Polly had insisted on Gwenda's stopping the car so that she could get out and add to her bunch some new blue flower she was puzzling over. She climbed the bank to get a good specimen and stung her bare legs on nettles. Gwenda sat in the car with her eyes closed.

Polly, having spat into her palm and rubbed it on her smarting legs, began to search for the blue flower in *Fleurs de Prés et des Bois*, instead of looking at the map. Crossroads were on them suddenly and she had no directions to give. Gwenda pulled to the side of the road, having taken the wrong turning, and reached for the map, screwing in her monocle. As she was studying it, frowning, or looking up at the sun for her bearings, Polly said, "I suppose it's a sort of campanula. What on earth does 'lancéolées' mean? Oh, I *wish* I'd brought my proper flower book from home."

"It's *this* road we want," Gwenda said, following it on the map with her nicotined finger. "If you could remember, we turn off *here*, and about eight kilometres further on bear right." She handed back the map. Polly had scarcely glanced at it, but she took it obediently, although she could never read it unless they were travelling north, which at present they were not.

"And when we've surmounted *that* little problem, you'd better look in the Michelin for somewhere for tonight," Gwenda added, and began to wrench the car round grimly, as if it were a five-ton lorry.

It was ten years since she had been in this part of France; with her husband then. They had travelled along the Dordogne Valley, from the mouth to the source, crossing from bank to bank. It was in the year that he died, and she remembered with a turn of her heart, how, as she was driving, she would give secret glances at him, knowing him so well that he could never hide the signs of pain coming on—the difference in breathing, the slight shifting in his seat, the hand going involuntarily to his chest, and then at once returning to his lap to grip hold of the map. He could read maps in whichever direction they were heading.

Polly had put the flower book into the dashboard pocket and had her head in the Michelin guide. She was dreadfully short-sighted, but would not wear spectacles, however much Gwenda nagged her. She would not even use the subterfuge of lenses in sun-glasses, which had been suggested.

"There's one with two pairs of those scissors at a place called—I think it's Sebonac."

"Selonac," Gwenda said. "How much?"

"I can't see."

"I'll have a look later. Can you find it on the map?"

"I already have," Polly said with pride.

Gwenda was always fussing about money—heading Polly off the Menu Gastronomique onto the eleven franc one. Although it was Polly's money, Polly sometimes thought.

Gwenda's husband had left her poorly provided for, and she had taken a job managing an hotel until Polly's mother, her own godmother, had begged her to look after Polly, *poor* Polly she always called her, and administer her affairs. This was before the operation from which she did not recover (as the doctor put it, but Gwenda did not), 'if anything should happen', as she put *that*. Polly was left very comfortable indeed. Long ago, people had thought Gwenda's parents clever to have chosen so rich a slight acquaintance to be Gwenda's Godmother.

As soon as Mrs Hervey had died, Gwenda moved into her place; into the house in Surrey—red brick with a green dome, monkey-puzzle trees and dark banks of rhododendrons, everywhere smelling of pine trees. Polly was acquiescent. She could not have managed on her own. This was clear to everyone. And at twenty-seven it was thought unlikely that she would marry. In spite of the solid worth of her position, men seemed uncertain with her, found her scatter-brained and childish conversation maddening, wondered amongst themselves if she were really all there. She was like a lanky child with her pale, freckled face, soft, untidy hair, her awkwardness. She was forever tripping over carpets or walking into doors. She got on people's nerves.

The responsibility of having quite a little heiress on her hands was one Gwenda felt she could shoulder. She was ready to deal with impoverished widowers or ambitious younger men; but few came their way in Surrey. Fork luncheons for women was their manner of entertaining, or an evening's bridge which Polly did not join in. She would sit apart, sticking foreign stamps crookedly into an album. Besides stamps, she collected Victorian bun pennies, lustre jugs, fans, sea-shells, match-boxes and pressed wild-flowers. There was a pile of albums full of pressed flowers, and what she seemed to love best about being in France was the chance of collecting different varieties. She hoped that Selonac, when they arrived there, would have more surprises. In a foreign country there was always the delight of not knowing what she might discover next— some rare strange orchid, perhaps, that she had never found before.

But Selonac was, at first sight, a disappointment—a few straggling houses on either side of the road. They were nearly through it when they saw a sign—'Auberge'— pointing down a lane to the right. "There!" shouted Polly, trying to be efficient, but Gwenda was already turning the corner. They came to a little cobbled *Place*, with a church and a baker's shop and a garage and the auberge—with one or two umbrellaed tables and some box trees in tubs on the pavement before it.

"I'll go and ask," Gwenda said. She always did all the fixing-up, while Polly sat mooning in the car over her wild-flowers, or squinting short-sightedly at the Guide Michelin, looking up for the twentieth time the difference between a black bath-tub and a white.

When Gwenda came back, she was followed by a young man, who dragged their suitcases out of the boot and lurched back into the darkness of the hotel with them.

It was a very dark and silent hotel. Polly felt depressed, as she went upstairs after Gwenda. She was never asked for her opinions about where they should stay. They never shared a room, and Gwenda always told her which was hers—and it was never the one nearest the bathroom or with the best view. She was glad that sharing a room was not one of Gwenda's economies. Gwenda snored like a man. She had heard her through many a thin wall.

This time they had the same view from their windows —across an orchard to a row of silvery trees which looked as if they bordered a stream. There was very little difference between the two rooms. Madame Peloux, the proprietress, showed Polly and Gwenda both, as if there were any chance of Polly making a choice; and then she began to chivvy her son, Jean, about the luggage. He was a clumsy, silent young man, and seemed to be sulking. His mother nagged him monotonously, as if from an old habit.

Like some wine, Polly did not travel well. She became more and more creased and greasy-faced. And the clothes in her suitcase, amongst the layers of tattered tissue-paper, all were creased, too, and all a little grubby, yet not *quite* grubby enough, she decided, to warrant all the fuss of getting them washed.

"Aren't you ready *yet*?" asked Gwenda at the door. "After all that driving, what I need is some *violent* exercise."

She usually said something like this, and once upon a time Polly had had amusing visions of her running across-country or playing a few chukkas of polo. Now she knew that all that would happen would be that Gwenda would drape her cardigan over her shoulders and go for a stroll round the garden, or amble round the village, stopping to look in shop-windows—longest at the charcuteries to marvel at terrines. She examined them with a professional eye; for her own pâté was quite the talk of their part of Surrey. When she was asked for the recipe, she became carefully vague and said she had none; that she just chucked in anything that came to hand.

This evening there was a pâté on the ten franc menu, so she was happy. She had had her stroll through the orchard, and Polly, still unpacking, had watched her from the bedroom window. Gwenda pushed her way through the long grass, lifting her neat ankles over briars. She had a top-heavy look, especially when viewed from above. Her large bosom was out of character, Polly thought. It was altogether too motherly-looking. And to think of Gwenda with children was impossible.

In the end, the unpacking was done, and the little walk was over, and they went into the almost empty dining-room. There were red and pink tablecloths, and large damp napkins to match, and Jean, Madame Peloux's son, had combed his frizzy hair, and was waiting inexpertly at table.

"Mosquitoes," Gwenda was saying. "I'm afraid there might be. I went up and closed the shutters."

There *was* a stream at the bottom of the orchard, across a narrow lane. She had come to it on her wanderings, and had been bitten a little by midges.

"The pâté's not bad," she said, dipping into the jar of gherkins.

Polly thought it a bit 'off'—well, sour anyway; but she said nothing. She was too often told that the taste she objected to was the very one that had been aimed at, the absolute perfection of flavour.

Jean annoyed Gwenda by saying the name of every-thing he put on the table—as if she and Polly were children. "Truites," he announced, setting the dish down. They looked delicious—sprinkled with parsley and shredded almonds.

Gwenda, whose French—like everything else—was so much better than Polly's, asked if they were from the stream below the orchard, and Jean looked evasive, as if he could not understand her. "Truites," he said again, and turned away, knocking over a glass as he did so.

The only other guests sat across the room. They were obviously not newcomers. They were favoured by the best table at the garden window, whereas Gwenda and Polly looked out onto the square. They had a bottle of wine with their name scribbled on the label, and the man poured it out himself, looking very serious as he did so. The woman drank water, holding the glass in a shaking hand, tinkling it against her false teeth. She was ancient. He was in his sixties, and she was his mother.

As they were French, Gwenda had to listen with a little extra concentration to what they said—although they said little, and that in muted voices, as they stared before them, waiting for Jean to bring the next dish.

The old woman was thin and ashen and wore a sort of half-mourning of grey and mauve, and a hat—a floppy, linen garden hat. The only real colour about her was her crimson shiny lips, crookedly done, which she kept pressed together, and smudged, after every sip of water, with a purple handkerchief. Large diamond rings kept slipping on her old fingers.

"Mother and son," Gwenda said in a low explanatory voice to Polly.

Jean had brought a tart to be cut from. Glazed slices of apple were slightly burnt. He made a great business of cutting their slices, frowning and pursing his lips as if it were a very tricky job.

Monsieur and Madame Devancourt, as he then addressed them, waved the tart away. Gwenda fastened on the name; repeated it once or twice in her mind, and had it secure.

"How *good* not to have anything frozen," she said, as she said at nearly every meal-time.

"The tart is lovely," Polly said. She loved sweet things, and longed for them through the other courses.

Madame Devancourt played with her rings and stared about her, while her tall, bald son was peeling an orange for her. They really were a very silent pair; but sometimes he made a little joke, and she gave a smothered snigger behind her handkerchief. It was surprising—sounded like a naughty little girl laughing in church.

Through the window, Polly watched one or two people sitting at the tables outside the inn, looking rather bored as they sipped their evening drink. A middle-aged woman, with a bitter, closed expression on her face, sat beside an older woman who was bowed-over, so hunch-backed that she kept losing balance and slipping sideways. Then the younger woman—she was obviously her daughter—would put her right, and turn her head away again, without a word. After a while, she suddenly stood up, got her mother to her feet and began a slow progress back across the *Place*.

Jean brought coffee to Gwenda and Polly and slopped it into the saucers pouring it out. Gwenda asked for another saucer and when he brought it, he looked so sulky that Polly smiled up at him, and thanked him in her atrocious accent. She knew so well herself what it was like to be clumsy and inadequate.

"Such a moron," Gwenda said. "Never mind, it's only for one night."

Although it turned out to be for six.

Gwenda always got up for breakfast. She found French beds uncomfortable, and 'liked to be about', as she put it.

The Devancourts were also up. Madame was wearing her floppy hat, and a pair of grubby tennis-shoes. Her son peeled another orange for her, and made a few more jokes. She seemed to be his life, and accepted his attentions placidly. But she was, in her own way, protective to *him*. When he half stood up, with his napkin in one hand and the orange in the other, and bowed to Gwenda and Polly as they came in, she stared hard at him, as if willing him back into his seat, and Polly could imagine her having guarded him from women since he was a young man, just as Gwenda had warded off young men from herself. When he had sat down again and resumed his careful orange-peeling, the old woman turned a cold and steady gaze on Gwenda, as if to say, "Don't waste any time on *this* one. He is mine." At Polly she did not so much as glance. Few people did. It was surprising that Jean darted forward and drew out her chair before he attended to Gwenda, although he shot it out so fast and so far that she almost fell on the floor.

"I really don't think he's all there," Gwenda said.

She had brought the maps down to breakfast, and said that she thought that they could get to the source of the river that day. It was so beautiful up there in the Auvergne, she said. The air so clear. The flowers so beautiful. At the thought of the flowers, Polly brightened; but there was also the thought of the day ahead, with all the difficulties of the map-reading and Gwenda's making a martyrdom of the driving—though it was she who forced the pace, who was determined to retrace every footstep of that last holiday with her husband. Why she wanted to do this, Polly found a puzzle—especially as that holiday must have been permeated with tragedy. Gwenda had always talked of it a great deal, and she talked of her husband more than Polly could endure. Such trivial repetitions—such as, every morning, "*How* Humphrey loved French bread!" and reminiscences all the way along the road. And there were implications that Polly knew none of the secret joys of matrimony, and would be unlikely ever to learn them. So Polly felt excluded, as well as bored.

Sometimes, alone in her bedroom, she lay for a little while face-down on the bed, upset by vague desires. If the desires were to be loved, she had no face to match her longing; simply nothing to define her day-dreams. "I want! I just *want!*" she sometimes moaned softly into the pillows.

"Oh, *lazy*-bones!" Gwenda would say, opening the door as she knocked on it. "Even at *my* age, I wouldn't dream of lying down in the daytime." As like as not, she would be on her way downstairs for some of her *violent* exercise. This morning, having mused once more on Humphrey's love of French bread, Gwenda put in her monocle and unfolded a map.

They were breakfasting in the bar, with a view through the open door across the *Place*. It was early in the morning, and children were gathered at the tables outside, waiting for the school bus. The boys smoked, and some of the older girls were playing a game of cards. They were very orderly, though gay, and made a sound like starlings. Gwenda kept glancing up in annoyance, and glaring through her monocle. Polly felt envious of the children.

Madame Devancourt padded past them in her tennis shoes, followed by her son. He bowed again, but she kept her eyes ahead. Presently, Jean appeared outside with a stiff broom and began to sweep between the tables; then he leaned on the broom and talked to some of the children; almost seeming to be one of them, without, for once, his shy or sullen look. Perhaps he too was envious of them, Polly thought.

"Jean, Jean!" Madame Peloux came in in her black overall and called her son's attention to his work, and he shrugged and glowered and began to sweep again.

The school bus came, was filled, and drove off, and there was silence except for the rasping of the broom on the pavement. When he had finished the sweeping, Jean watered the box-shrubs and a sharp, cold smell cut off the heat of the morning for a while.

"Have you packed?" Gwenda asked Polly, knowing that she had not.

As Polly got up, she bumped against the table, and

Gwenda looked up sharply and clicked her tongue. Polly, catching Jean's eyes, blushed, ashamed to be rebuked in front of him. He was standing in the doorway, flicking the last drops from the watering-can about the pavement.

As she went upstairs, Polly thought, I'll bet old Humphrey never bumped into things, and she hoped for his sake that he hadn't.

Gwenda paid the bill, then she walked about the court-yard, smoking to soothe herself. The exasperation she felt at having to wait always for Polly was a trembling pain. She hated to wait, and now spent hours of her life doing so. She herself was quick and decisive, always thinking one step ahead. Routine things, like packing, for instance, were so boring that she would get them done with great speed, only to waste time she had saved pacing up and down while Polly dithered.

Jean brought down her case and put it in the boot of the car.

Monsieur Devancourt came out to the garage with his fishing-rods. He stopped to wish Gwenda a pleasant journey, then drove off in his old and dusty Citroën. As Gwenda looked back to the inn for any sign of Polly, she saw old Madame Devancourt, still wearing her hat, staring down at her from a window.

Already the sun was strong. Smells of baking came through the kitchen window, and Gwenda began to long for the cool air of the Auvergne.

At last Jean brought down Polly's suitcase, and Polly followed soon after. Madame Peloux came out from the kitchen, wiping her floury hands on her apron.

As they drove out of the courtyard, Polly thought, "As

soon as I get to like a place, we have to move on," and she turned back and waved to Jean, who was staring after them in his vacant way.

But Gwenda was insistent on moving on, on retracing every mile of her holiday with Humphrey. They had to get up to the source and back through Northern France, and there were only ten days left. Then Gwenda had to go home to open a garden fête.

"I love this feeling of starting out fresh in the mornings," she said, as they drove out of the square. "Humphrey used to say . . ." She slowed down, reaching the main road; the engine stalled, and stopped, and would not start again.

"Oh, drat it," said Gwenda.

Now the heat poured into the car. While Gwenda tugged at the starter and made her mild, but furious-sounding imprecations, Polly placidly looked at her wild-flower book, as if the hitch did not involve her, and would soon be put right.

Jean, who had watched the car and seen it stop, came running towards them. He opened the bonnet and seemed to take a very grave view. After a while he fetched his friend from the garage. The car was towed away, and Gwenda and Polly decided to return temporarily to the auberge and drink a citron pressé.

"Now, we shall have a job to get to the mountains by this evening," Gwenda said.

Polly was playing with a cat.

As the day went on, the idea of the mountains receded. Jean carried their suitcases back upstairs, and they unpacked.

"A week at *least*," Gwenda moaned. "And if they *say*

that, goodness only knows what it might really mean. Stuck in this place."

"It's quite a *nice* place," said Polly.

"Yes, but it's not what we planned."

The car was in the village garage, and a spare part had been telephoned for, and for once there seemed nothing that Gwenda could do. So she went to lie down, in the heat of the afternoon—the thing she said she never did. Polly, at a loose end, wandered in the orchard, looking for flowers. It was like the afternoons of her childhood, when her mother rested, and she was left to her own devices. In those days, she had felt under a spell. Through an open window she could hear the solid ticking of a grandfather-clock and on the terrace, the peacocks squawked with a sound of rusty shears being forced open. Here there was only the busy noise of the cicadas in the grass.

At the bottom of the orchard, she saw Jean. He was beckoning to her eagerly, and she hurried forward, with a wading motion, through the long grass. He had few words to say—from habit, from gaucherie, from fear of her foreignness. To make up for his dumbness, his gestures were all exaggerated, like Harpo Marx's. They came out of the orchard and crossed the narrow, gritty lane, which was lanced by sunlight striking through birch trees.

With a complete disregard for Polly's bare legs, he took her hand and drew her through looped and tangled brambles, disturbing dozens of small blue butterflies. Polly could hear the stream, but not see it for all the under-growth. She wondered where they were going, and what all the secrecy and haste and excitement were about. Jean parted some reeds and she could see the stream again. It

looked less deep than it was, for it was very clear, and the
fat brown stones on its bed seemed near the surface. Jean
turned and lifted Polly with his hands round her waist.
He swung her down over the bank onto a boulder. It had
seemed a sudden, reckless thing to do and her breath was
taken away; but she landed quite safely on the boulder,
with his large rough hands steadying her.

He became more secretive than ever, carefully drawing
aside branches to show to her a part of the stream, caged
off by wire netting. The water flowed through the trap,
which was full of trout, turning back and forth, and swimming as best they could. So this was his secret? Polly smiled,
and he watched her face intently, and when she turned to
him and nodded—she knew not why—he put a finger to
his lips and narrowed his eyes. To an onlooker they would
have seemed like people in a silent movie.

For a moment or two, they stood in contemplation,
hypnotised by the slowly moving fish; then, suddenly,
with more frantic gestures, Jean dashed off again. He took
a spade from a hiding-place under a bush and began to try
to thrust it into the earth. Polly turned to watch him with
amazement. The earth was hard. He lifted a piece of rough
turf and bent to examine the soil, clicking his tongue in
disapproval. In spite of the dryness of the earth, he managed, as he dug deeper, to find a few worms. He brought
them eagerly to Polly and put them into the palm of her
hand, as if they were a handful of precious stones. She
recoiled, but he did not notice and, to show her how, he
took one of the worms from her and tore it into pieces and
threw them to the fish. With a feeling of revulsion, Polly
flung her handful suddenly into the trap. Some fell through,

others lay on the wire-netting, writhing. She bent down and dipped her hand into the cool water, while Jean poked at the worms with a stick, clicking his tongue in vexation.

"Jean! Jean!" They could hear his mother calling him across the orchard.

He frowned. He watched the trout a little longer, then he seemed to gather himself from a trance, braced himself, and gave his hands to Polly, dragging her clumsily up the bank. "Jean! Jean!" the voice went on calling, getting shriller. He looped briars carefully over the trap and he and Polly set off.

Madame Peloux was standing in the orchard. She waved a basket at them, for there was some errand for Jean to run — he had to go to the farm to fetch a chicken for dinner. An old boiler, she explained rapidly, aside from Polly.

Polly stood, hesitating, unsure whether to walk on or not. Then, feeling very bold and having composed the sentence in French before she spoke it, she asked if she might go with him to the farm. His face at once lost its sulkiness, and the errand seemed to take on a bright aspect. Madame Peloux stood looking suspiciously after them as they set off.

"What *has* come over you?" Gwenda asked Polly, fearing that she knew. She had found the girl sitting by her bedroom window, studying a phrase-book. It was opened at *Le Marché*.

"You always said I should improve my French," Polly replied defensively.

"But you never cared to try, did you? Before?"

It was a brilliant early evening, and Gwenda had looked in on her way downstairs. In the garden the acacias were full of sunlight against the pale blue sky. Martins and swallows darted about the terra-cotta, crenellated out-house roof, catching, Gwenda hoped, the mosquitoes which otherwise might have plagued her later. There was a smell of lime-blossom and honeysuckle and, down below, in the vegetable-garden lilies grew like weeds.

"I could stay here for ever, I think," Polly said, glancing across the orchard.

"This was hardly the object of our holiday," Gwenda said. She was fretful to complete their journey. She talked continually of getting to the source, to the mountains, so infuriatingly near, where she and Humphrey had been so happy. As they were arrested on their travels, there were no fresh sights to discuss, so she talked about Humphrey, and Polly wished that she would not. Gwenda spoke of marriage as if it were something exclusive to herself and her late husband. She referred to past experiences, implying that Polly would never know similar ones.

"Humphrey and I climbed right to the summit," she said. "There was an enormous view, and gentians—great patches of gentians."

"I should love to see gentians," Polly said.

"Well, I doubt if we shall now," Gwenda said briskly. "It's so infuriating. You really ought not to read that small print. Your nose almost touches the page. So ridiculous. We shall have to see about getting you some spectacles when we get back."

"I shan't wear them," Polly said, in a mild but firm voice. Sometimes, quietly, she put her foot down, and then

Gwenda let the matter go. It was such a rare occurrence that it did not constitute a threat. All the same, only that morning Polly had insisted on going to the market with Jean, and had left Gwenda at the garage and gone on with him alone. Gwenda was always at the garage, making the same complaints, asking the same questions.

"You'll find you'll come to them in the end," she said, referring to the spectacles. "Now do take your head out of that book, there's a dear girl. Let's go down and have a drink. I promised the Devancourts we'd join them."

Madame Devancourt now seemed warmly disposed to them. She had decided that they were lesbians, and so of no danger to her son. Passing their table at breakfast, the day after the breakdown, the old lady had commiserated with them. She was formal and condescending. By dinner-time, she had warmed a little more; and the following morning had come to them, with her son hovering behind her, to invite them to a drive out in the afternoon. "Having no car you will see nothing of our country," she said.

So they had driven out along rutted, dusty lanes to see a small château. It stood high on a slope over the river, bone-white, with black candle-snuffer turrets. Madame Devancourt had the name of a friend to mention, and the housekeeper admitted them. The family was away, and she went ahead from room to room, opening shutters, drawing dust-covers from furniture, lifting drugget from needle-work carpets. There were some portraits, some pieces of tapestry, deer's heads and antlers growing from almost every wall, and a chilly smell from the stone floors. Madame Devancourt and Gwenda exclaimed over everything, drew one another to view this and that treasure or curiosity.

Each was impressed by the other's knowledge. Monsieur Devancourt looked out of the windows, and Polly trailed behind, immeasurably bored.

She regretted this new friendship. Gwenda's fluency with French debarred Polly from any part in the conversation—not that she had anything to say. She was frightened of the old lady, and thought her son a pitiful creature. Now they must spend an hour with them sitting under the umbrellas outside the auberge. She took her wild-flower book with her, and looked for a picture of a gentian. "Gentiane," said Jean, pointing at the illustration, when he had set down her drink before her.

"Oui," she said, smiling and blushing.

"Oui, gentiane," he repeated, turning to take an order from another table.

"He will drive me *mad*," said Gwenda.

Then there was the little commotion of having to get up as Madame Devancourt shuffled out to join them, her son following, carrying her handbag and her cardigan.

At another table came the other sorry pair, the habituées, the crippled mother and the bitter-faced daughter. Every evening, they sat for twenty minutes in the *Place*. The daughter sipped a drink, and kept propping up her mother. Not a word was spoken. When it was time to go, the daughter stood up in silence and helped her mother to her feet, and then to go slowly across the square. Homewards. Polly tried not to imagine any more—the dreadful ritual of getting mother to bed. All old, she thought, looking round her. Whenever Jean passed by, he nodded his head at her, as if he were saying, "Ah, yes, you're still there."

Gwenda, missing nothing, frowned.

He continued to madden her through dinner. When he brought the trout, he winked at Polly, collusively.

"One can grow tired even of trout," Gwenda complained. "Every evening. I do wish, Polly, you would try to ignore that terrible young man. He is quite oafish. I would have said he winked at you just now, if I could believe it possible."

She had ordered a bottle of wine to be put on the Devancourts' table—a token of gratitude for their kindness—and now Monsieur Devancourt across the room raised his glass in a courtly gesture, and Madame her glass of water, with a shaking hand.

"Very affy," said Polly in a low voice.

After dinner, the four of them sat in the stuffy little salon, and Gwenda told them stories about her husband.

"Excuse me," Polly murmured, slipping away suddenly —the very thing Gwenda had been determined she should not do.

In the courtyard, Jean was watering the tubs of geraniums. The air had a delicious smell.

At once, before Gwenda could find an excuse to come after them, he put down the watering-can and they set off across the orchard. Every evening he went to the stream to clean the trout-trap of drifting weeds and sticks and to dig up worms. They said very little—although Polly persevered with a few short sentences, and sometimes Jean pointed at plants and trees and said their name clearly in French, which she obediently repeated.

Although he was clumsy and unpredictable and could not speak a word of her language, Polly felt safe and at home with him. There was never anyone young in her life

—neither here nor at home. She liked to go shopping with him in the market. It was the simplest, poorest of markets. Old women sat patiently beside whatever they had for sale—a few broad beans tied in a bundle, a live duck in a basket, lime-flowers for tisane, a bucketful of arum lilies or Canterbury bells. She and Jean went from one to the other, comparing cheeses, and pressing the bean-pods, and she felt a sense of intimacy, as if they were playing a game of being husband and wife. Nothing Gwenda could say would prevent her from going to the market.

This evening, she helped him to clean the trap, she fed worms to the fish, having lost her squeamishness. They were as busy and absorbed as children.

Throwing the last worm, she lost her balance on the boulder, and one foot went into the water; but he was there at once to steady her. She was annoyed with herself, wondering how to explain to Gwenda her soaking wet sandal, without revealing the secret of this place.

Jean lifted her up and sat her on the bank.

"I shall stay here for a while," she said. Perhaps Gwenda would go up to bed early, although more likely not.

He understood her, and sat down beside her, feeling worried, because soon his mother would be calling "Jean! Jean!" all round the garden—there would be some job to be done.

When they had been together before, there had always been something to be busy about—the marketing, the fish. Now each had only the other one in mind. He sat there staring in front of him, as if he were wondering what on earth to do next, for he had scarcely been allowed five minutes idleness in his life. Then he suddenly had an inspiration. He turned and kissed her suddenly on the side of her face, then, less awkwardly, on her forehead. Polly had been kissed only by her mother and elderly relations; but she felt that she knew more about it than Jean. She put her hands behind his head and kissed him very strongly on the mouth. She felt quite faint with delight. But hardly had they had any time to enjoy their kissing, when that far-off, coming and going, mosquito-plaint began—"Jean! Jean!"—across the orchard.

Until they were in sight of the house, they went hand in hand, saying nothing. Although the kissing was over, something remained—an excitement, a gladness. Something Gwenda, surely, could never have experienced.

That Gwenda guessed something of what had happened was shown by her coldness and huffiness. She had felt awkward, sitting in the salon with the Devancourts. Polly had excused herself so abruptly, and Madame Devancourt kept looking towards the door. Gwenda was glad when, at their usual time, Monsieur Devancourt fetched the draughtboard and set out the counters. She watched for a little while, and realised that the son was making stupid mistakes so that his mother could win. Then, hearing Madame Peloux outside, calling for Jean, Gwenda got up uneasily, and said that she was going to have an early night. She went upstairs and threw open the window, regardless of mosquitoes.

Polly and Jean were coming back across the orchard. Gwenda began to shake violently, and moved back a few steps from the window. Jean answered his mother, but did not say a word to Polly, not even when she turned away from him to enter the house.

Gwenda was so unpleasantly disturbed that she felt unable to face Polly, and dreaded her coming to say goodnight. But she did not come. The footsteps stopped at the next room, and Gwenda heard the door open, and then shut. This was something that had never happened before. There were too many things happening for the first time. Gwenda lay in bed worrying about them, and she slept badly.

At breakfast, nothing was right. She snapped at Jean for slopping the coffee, she complained that the butter was rancid, and she found every word that Polly said in French excruciating. "Your command of the language grows as fast as your accent deteriorates." She preferred the days when Polly did not try, and had no reason for doing so. "Whatever must the Devancourts think? They must wonder where on earth you picked up such an accent."

"It's not *for* them to wonder," Polly said calmly. "They can't speak a *word* of English."

She *was* calm. She was *too* calm, Gwenda decided. And Jean did not look at her this morning, nor she at him. It seemed to Gwenda that they no longer felt they needed to.

"Oh, *damn* the car," she suddenly said.

Polly looked a little surprised, but said nothing.

"I think I'll have a look round the market this morning," Gwenda said casually.

The three of them later set off, and there was only a brief chance to make an assignation, when Gwenda almost instinctively paused to look at a terrine on a stall.

The friendship with the Devancourts played into Polly's

hands. Just at the right moment of the afternoon, Madame Devancourt came downstairs with a photograph-album to show to Gwenda—her collection of photographs of great houses, all to be gone over and explained in detail, trapping Gwenda who thought that she would scream. Monsieur Devancourt was attending to his fishing-tackle, so the two women were left alone, sitting in the stuffy salon. It was too hot to go out-of-doors, Madame Devancourt said.

Polly, who had gone into the lavatory, to try to plan her escape, saw the delightful sight of Gwenda with the album on her knees and Madame Devancourt leaning over, pointing at a photograph with a shaking finger. She slipped away without being seen. Jean, whose slack time it was, was waiting for her by the trout-trap. He pulled briars and bracken round them, like a nest and, without much being said, made love to her.

The old lady smelled of camphor and lavender. She leant so close that Gwenda almost choked. Sometimes little flecks of spit fell on the pages of the album, and were quickly wiped away with the purple handkerchief. Gwenda tried to turn the pages quickly, but this would not do; for every coign and battlement and drawbridge had to be explained.

At last Monsieur Devancourt interrupted them. He had finished with his fishing-tackle and had come to take them for a little drive. Where was Mademoiselle Polly, he wondered. Gwenda flushed, and said that she must be writing letters in her room; and she excused herself from the outing, having a headache, she explained.

When they had gone, Gwenda walked up and down the garden-path. She strutted, with rather apart legs, like a starling. She listened and she looked about her. But there were no voices. It was a hot, humming afternoon. The Devancourts' car went off, and then there was nothing but the sound of insects, and hardly a leaf moved.

"Her mother!" Gwenda kept saying to herself. "What would her mother think?"

It was a real headache she had, and the sun was making it much worse. It drove her inside—up to the vantage-point of her bedroom-window.

It was a long time before she saw Polly coming back across the orchard. She walked slowly, and was alone. But that was only a ruse, a piece of trickery, Gwenda was sure.

She leaned out of the window and called to her.

Polly seemed to come unwillingly, and stood hesitating at Gwenda's door.

"Where have you been?"

"For a walk."

"With that dreadful loutish youth."

Polly pressed her lips together.

"He's not even . . ." Gwenda shrugged and turned aside; and after a few moments in which nothing else was said, Polly went quietly to her own room. Although she foresaw all the agonising awkwardness of the rest of the holiday—even, vaguely, of the rest of her life (Gwenda going on being huffy in Surrey)—she dismissed its importance. She stood before the looking-glass, combing her hair dreamily, staring at her freckled face with its band of sun-burn across the forehead. It was she now, she decided, who had something exclusively her own, and it seemed to her that

Gwenda had nothing—for even her memories were threadbare.

In the night, just before dawn, Gwenda woke up. Something had disturbed her, and she lay listening. There was silence, save for far-away cow-bells occasionally heard. then a floor-board creaked on the landing, and another. There was a gentle tapping on a bedroom door, and whispering.

She felt very cold, and sick, and deceived. She groped for her watch and peered at its luminous dial. It was nearly five o'clock. There was no real light in the sky, but perhaps a lessening of darkness.

Boards now creaked quite heavily along the passage, down the stairs. Gwenda got out of bed and went to the window, gently easing the shutters apart. As she did so, she heard an outside door open, and then a man's voice, speaking in low tones just below her. As her eyes grew used to the dark, she could make out two figures. After a moment, they moved off towards the courtyard, and she could see then that they were Jean and Monsieur Devancourt, both carrying fishing-rods. After a while, she heard the car starting up. It drove away, and she listened to it fading into the distance. Then the church clock struck five.

She left the shutters opened, and got back into bed. The sky slowly lightened, and she turned about heavily on the rough, darned sheets, longing for day to come so that she could get on with it, hasten through it. She searched her mind for plans for escaping from this hated place and, faced with all the complications, found none.

At breakfast, Gwenda was tired and silent. She seemed to brood over her coffee, staring before her, the drooping lines of her face deeper than ever. Monsieur Devancourt and Jean returned, having caught a large pike. Jean quickly slipped on a white jacket and brought fresh coffee. Monsieur Devancourt joined his mother, and peeled her orange for her, was full of simple triumph at his successful expedition, and now wanted nothing but to devote the rest of the day to her. They discussed their plans with great pleasure.

As usual, Madame Devancourt stopped on her way past Gwenda's and Polly's table.

"How early a riser would it be possible for you to be?" she asked. She seemed playful, like a child with a secret. She hardly waited for Gwenda's reply. "Then," she went on, "we have a little plan, Louis and I. We know your disappointment at not reaching the source of the river, and we think that if we can start early tomorrow we can make the journey and spend the following night en route. It would give us great pleasure. How does it strike you?"

It struck Gwenda very well, and she said so. She brightened at once. Polly, who never understood what Madame Devancourt said, had not tried to listen. When it was explained to her, she was appalled, and too artless to hide the fact. Gwenda touched her foot under the table to bring her to her senses; but she could only stammer her thanks, while looking quite dismayed.

"But it's dreadful for *me*," she complained to Gwenda afterwards. "I can't understand a single word they say. To have a long drive like that with them!"

She knew that she would have to go. She was not strong

enough to resist Gwenda over this. After a while she forgot what was hanging over her. She was living in the present, and it was time to go to market with Jean. Gwenda, more relaxed now, let them go alone, while she visited the garage and made another fuss.

The next day, they left very early. Jean was up before them and brought them coffee and bread. It was a strange, cold dawn, and they moved about quietly, with lowered voices, putting things into the boot of the car. At the last moment, Polly found she had forgotten her wild-flower book and had to get out of the car and go and find it. It was her only solace—and such a small one to her in her altered life—that she might see gentians growing in the mountains. Jean stood ready to open the car-door for her when she returned. His eyes rested mournfully upon her. As they drove off, she could see him standing there, staring after her, looking sulky.

Madame Devancourt was quite talkative this morning. She sat in front beside her son, and half turned her wedge-shaped face back towards Gwenda. Polly she completely ignored. She thought her an imbecile and wondered that Gwenda had not found a more intelligent and presentable partner. It seemed to her that they were not so very much in love, though in such cases, she found it difficult to tell.

They stopped for lunch at an inn full of memories for Gwenda. She was delighted. Her spirits had been rising all morning, as they climbed higher into the colder air. She became animated, and infected Madame Devancourt with her liveliness. Both had such recollections—and all along the route the two widows exchanged them. La Bourboule! Le mont-Dore! There were changes to be noted. Yet so much had remained the same. Monsieur Devancourt listened to them as he drove, smiling to see his mother so gay. It was unusual for her to have feminine companionship, and it seemed to do her good. Polly stared at the wild-flowers along the way. She was obviously not allowed to stop to gather them. Monsieur Devancourt sometimes addressed a remark to her and then she started out of her dreams and became confused, and Gwenda had to rescue her.

After lunch, they went on to the source. The river they had driven beside became, at last, a thin fast trickle down the mountain-side. The road ended. They got out of the car and felt the air cold on their faces, and Polly looked about for flowers. The gentians were higher up, Gwenda told her, and she said that she for one was determined to climb to the summit, as she and Humphrey had done. They could be taken nearly there in the funicular.

Madame Devancourt declined. She would sit in the car and wait for them, and be quite happy reading her novel, she explained.

"Your mother is charming," Gwenda told Monsieur Devancourt as they waited for the lift to come down.

"It is altogether a charming day," he said.

As they were hauled up by the cable-car, Polly, although dizzy, peered down at the rocks for flowers. She saw miniature daffodils, drifts of white anemones, and then, in a crevice, a patch of gentians. The funicular swung high above them and came to a stop.

This much higher up, it was windy. Strands of hair kept

lashing her cheeks. She hated the wind, and she hated being so high. Above them, at the top of a zig-zagging path, she could see two tiny figures waving from the highest rock.

"I shouldn't like to go up there," she said to Gwenda.

"But that's why we've come," Gwenda said with a tone of scorn. "Humphrey . . ." Then she changed her mind about what she was going to say. She would climb to the summit alone with Monsieur Devancourt and say not a word about her husband all the way.

Polly, on this lower slope was quite content to scramble about and pick flowers. The tiny daffodils were exquisite, and there were varieties she could not classify until she got back to the car and found them in her book. But she could find no gentians. They seemed to grow in rockier parts. Here, there was only shabby, wind-bitten grass and patches of dirty snow. Barbed-wire ran along the edge of the ridge. Beyond it rocks went sheer down to the valley.

From the summit, Gwenda and Monsieur Devancourt, rather out-of-breath, paused triumphantly and looked about them at the wide view. They could see Polly below, darting like a child or a bee, from one flower to another, and they called to her, but their voices were snatched out of their throats by the wind. Then Gwenda began to shout in earnest, for she could see that Polly was trying to crawl under the barbed wire. She was lying on her stomach, reaching for something. Gwenda and Monsieur Devancourt called out in warning and began to scramble down the slippery path as quickly as they could. Before they could come within Polly's hearing, there was a dreadful rushing noise of bouncing and cascading scree, of rocks dropping with an echo upon other rocks. The noise continued long

after Polly had disappeared and Gwenda and Monsieur
Devancourt had come to the newly-opened fissure. Beside
it was a handful of flowers, and a piece of gentian-blue
chocolate-paper which Polly must have been reaching for.

Monsieur Devancourt had been a tower of strength. He
had interviewed police officials and undertakers, inter-
cepted newspaper-men, booked the flight home, arranged
about the coffin, sent telegrams, and brought Gwenda back
to Selonac to pack the cases. And every now and then he
bewailed the fact that the tragic excursion had been his idea.

Gwenda was stunned, rather than grief-stricken. She
leaned on his kindness. She let him do everything for her.

Madame Devancourt now seemed to have withdrawn.
Her son's solicitude was irksome and disturbing, and looks
of suspicion were cast on him and Gwenda. The episode
had been distasteful, encroaching—and she had had
enough of her, this Englishwoman, with her demanding
ways. Instead of taking command, as one of her kind
should have done, she had clung to a man like any silly
girl.

"I can never say 'thank you' enough," Gwenda said.
She had come to them in the salon to bid them goodbye.
"When you visit England, I hope you will stay with
me, in my house in Surrey."

Madame Devancourt nodded forbiddingly; but Gwenda
hardly noticed. In her mind, she was introducing Monsieur
Devancourt—he had asked her to call him 'Louis'—to
her friends. "Do you play bridge?" she very nearly asked
him; but she stopped herself in time. She shook hands.

Once more Louis blamed himself for Polly's death, and his mother clicked her tongue impatiently.

Out in the courtyard, the car was waiting—ready at last; ready too late—and Jean was packing the cases into the boot. Gwenda had forgotten all about him. Madame Peloux stood by to wish her 'Bon Voyage'.

She looked into her bag for a tip, and advanced with it folded in her hand, ready to slip it into Jean's. He slammed down the lid of the boot and, as Gwenda came up to him, he turned sulkily aside, and walked away.

His face was swollen; he made a blubbering noise, like a miserable child and, going faster and faster, made off across the orchard.

"Ah, Jean! Jean!" his mother said, with a sigh and a shake of her head, looking after him.

Gwenda got into the car. It started perfectly. She waved to Madame Peloux and to Louis Devancourt, who had come out of the inn to watch her go, and drove away, towards the airport.

Tall Boy

THIS Sunday had begun well, by not having begun too early. Jasper Jones overslept—or, rather, slept later than usual, for there was nothing to get up for—and so had got for himself an hour's remission from the Sunday sentence. It was after half-past ten and he had escaped, for one thing, the clatter of the milk-van, a noise which for some reason depressed him. But church bells now began to toll—to him an even more dispiriting sound, though much worse in the evening.

The curtains drawn across the window did not meet. At night, they let a steamy chink of light out onto the darkness, and this morning let a grey strip of daylight in.

Jasper got out of bed and went to this window. It was high up in the house, and a good way down below, in the street, he could see some children playing on the crumbling front steps, and two women, wearing pale, tinselly saris and dark overcoats, hurrying along on the other side of the road.

In this part of London, nationalities clung together— Poles in one street, African negroes in the next. This road —Saint Luke's—was mostly Pakistani. Jasper thought he was the only West Indian all the way along it. *His* people were quite distant—in the streets near the railway-bridge, where the markets were, where he had been unable to find a room.

This bed-sitter was his world. There was distinction in having it all to himself. In such a neighbourhood, few did.

He had never in his life known such isolation. Back in his own country, home had bulged with people—bread-winners or unemployed, children, the elderly helpless—there was never an empty corner or time of real silence.

White people and coloured people now walked in twos and threes along Saint Luke's Road to the church on the corner. The peal of bells jangled together, faltered, then faded. Church-goers stepped up their pace. The one slow bell began and, when that stopped, the road was almost empty. For a time, there were only the children below playing some hopping game up and down the steps.

It was a very wide road. Fifty years ago, all those four-storeyed houses had been lived in by single families—with perhaps a little servant girl sleeping in an attic—in a room on the same floor as Jasper's. The flights of broken front steps led up to the porches with scabby pillars and—always—groups of dirty milk bottles. The sky was no-colour above the slate roofs and chimney-pots and tele-vision aerials, and the street looked no-colour, too—the no-colour of most of Jasper's Sunday mornings in London. Either the sky pressed down on him, laden with smog or rain or dark, lumbering clouds, or it vanished, it simply wasn't there, was washed away by rain, or driven some-where else by the wind.

He was bored with the street, and began to get dressed. He went down several times to the lavatory on the half-landing, but each time the door was bolted. He set about shaving—trimming his moustache neatly in a straight line well above his full, up-tilted lip. He washed a pair of socks and some handkerchiefs. When he had dusted the window, he spread the wet handkerchiefs, stretched and smoothed, against the pane to dry, having no iron. Then—in between times he was trying the lavatory door without luck —he fried a slice of bread in a little black pan over the gas-ring and, when it was done, walked about the room eating it, sometimes rubbing the tips of his greasy fingers in his frizzy hair, which was as harsh as steel wool.

He was a tall, slender young man, and his eyes had always looked mournful, even when he was happier, though hungry, at home in his own country. Tomorrow, he would be twenty-six. He remained, so far, solitary, worked hard, and grieved hard over his mistakes. He saved, and sent money back home to Mam. Poverty from the earliest days—which makes some spry and crafty—had left him diffident and child-like.

At last—having found the lavatory door open—he set out for his usual Sunday morning walk. People were coming out of Saint Luke's, standing in knots by the porch, taking it in turns to shake hands with the Vicar. Their clothes—especially the women's—were dauntingly respectable. One Sunday, Jasper had rather fearfully gone to the service, but the smell of damp stone, the mumbled, hurried prayers, the unrhythmical rush and gabble of psalms dismayed him. He had decided that this sense of alienation was one he could avoid.

Pubs had just opened, and he went into one—The Victoria & Albert—and ordered a glass of beer. This he did for passing time and not for enjoyment. Sweet, thick drinks were too expensive, and this warmish, wry-tasting one for which he tried to acquire a liking, was all he could afford. It made him wonder about Londoners, though, as that church service had. There seemed to be inherent in

them a wish for self-punishment he could not understand
—a greyness of soul and taste, to match the climate. Perhaps in total depression there was safety. His own depression—of fits and starts—held danger in it, he guessed.

The barman went round the tables collecting glasses,
carrying away five in each hand, fingers hooked into them.
The pub was filling up. As soon as the door swung to, it
was pushed open again. After a time, people coming in
had rain on their shoulders, and wiped it from their faces.
The sight of this was a small calamity to Jasper, who had
planned to spend at least half an hour queasily sipping
his beer. Now he would have to drain his glass quickly
and go, because of his shoes and the need to have them
dry for the morning—and his suit.

The rain brushed the streets, swept along by the wind.
He changed into a run, shoulders high and his head held
back to stop the rain running down his spine, so that it
spurted instead from his eyelids and his moustache. His
arms going like pistons, his knees lifted high, he loped
slowly easily. In one way, he loved and welcomed the
rain, for giving him the chance to run. He always wanted
to run, but people stared when he did so, unless he were
running for a bus. Running for running's sake was an
oddity. He was worried only about his suit and shoes, and
the shoes were already soaked, and there was a soapy
squelch in his socks.

He reached home, panting and elated, and sprang lightly
up the three flights of stairs. When he had hung up his
damp suit and put on his working overalls, stuffed his wet
shoes with newspaper and set them to dry, soles facing
the gas-ring, steaming faintly, he began to mix up his

dinner. Two rashers of bacon went into the frying-pan, then he took a handful or two of flour and rubbed in some dripping. He shaped the dough carefully into balls with his long, pale-palmed hands, and put them into the bacon fat. They were as near as he could get to his mother's fried dumplings. Perhaps, just at this moment, she would be making them at home, dumplings and sweet potato pudding. He imagined home having the same time as England. He would have felt quite lost to his loved ones if, when he woke in the night, he could not be sure that they were lying in darkness, too; and, when his own London morning came, theirs also came, the sun streamed through the cracks of their hut in shanty-town, and the little girls began to chirp and skip about. He could see them clearly now, as he knelt by the gas-ring—their large, rolling eyes, their close-cropped, frizzy hair. Most of the time, they had bare patches on their scalps from sores they would not leave alone, those busy fingers scratching, slapped down by Mam. They all had names of jewels, or semi-precious stones—Opal, Crystal, and Sapphyra, his little sisters. He smiled, and gently shook his head, as he turned the dumplings with a fork.

All the afternoon, the rain flew in gusts against the window. If he could not go out and walk about the streets, there was nothing to do. He took the chair to the window, and looked through the blurred pane at the street below; but there was no life down there—only an occasional umbrella bobbing along, or a car swishing by slowly, throwing up puddle-water with a melancholy sound.

The launderette round the corner was open on Sunday afternoons and evenings, and sometimes he took his dirty shirts and overalls and sat there before the washing-machine, waiting, his hands hanging loose between his knees, and the greenish, fluorescent light raining down on him. He might make a dash towards it, if the rain eased up a little. His heart began to ache for the bright launderette, as if for a dear dream.

Half-way through the afternoon, he quite suddenly experienced utter desolation. He knew the signs of it coming, and he closed his eyes and sat warily still, feeling silence freezing in his ear-drums. Then he got up quietly and began to pad up and down the room; stopping at the far wall from the window, he leant against the wall and rhythmically banged his forehead against it, his eyes shut tight again, his lips parted. Very soon, a sharp rapping came back from the other side—his only human recognition of the day. He reeled away from the wall, and sat on the edge of the bed, sighing dramatically, for something to do.

What light there had been during the day seemed to be diminishing. Time was going. Sunday was going. He lay on his back on the bed, while the room darkened, and he counted his blessings—all off by heart, he knew them well. There was nothing wrong. He was employed. He had a room, and a good suit, and his shoes would soon be dry. There was money going back home to Mam. No one here, in England, called him 'Nigger', or put up their fists to him. That morning, he had sat there in the pub without trouble. There *was* no trouble. Once, at work, they had all laughed at him when he was singing, *I'm Dreaming of a White Christmas*, as he loaded a van; but it was good-humoured laughter. *Tall Boy* they called him; but they had nick-names for some of the others, too—Dusty and Tiny and Buster.

Jasper thought about each of them in turn, trying to picture their Sundays from Monday morning chat that he always listened to carefully. The single ones tinkered with their motor-bikes, then went out on them, dressed in black mock leather, with a white-helmeted girl on the pillion. The married ones mended things, and put up shelves, they "went over to Mother's to tea", and looked at the telly as soon as the religious programmes were over. Dusty had even built a greenhouse in his back-garden, and grew chrysanthemums. But, whatever they did, all were sorry when Monday morning came. They had not longed for it since Friday night, as Jasper had.

The rain fell into the dark street. Whether it eased up or not, he had to catch the last post. He fetched pen and ink and the birthday-card for himself that he had chosen with great care, gravely conscious of the rightness of receiving one. He dipped the pen in the ink, then sat back, wondering what to write. He would have liked to sign it, 'From a well-wisher', as if it were to come out of the blue; but this seemed insincere, and he prized sincerity. After a while, he simply wrote, 'With greetings from Mr Jasper Jones', stamped the envelope, and went again to the window to look at his Sunday enemy, the rain.

In the end, he had to make a dash for it, splashing up rain from the wet pavements as he ran with long, loose strides through the almost deserted streets.

He thought Monday morning tea-break talk the best

of the week. He could not sincerely grouse with the others about beginning work again, so he listened happily to all they had to say. This had a comforting familiarity, like his dreams of home—the game of darts, the fish-and-chips, Saturday night at White City, and *Sunday Night at the Palladium* on telly while the children slap-dashed through the last of their homework; beef was roasted, a kitchen chair repainted and a fuse mended, mother-in-law was visited; someone had touched a hundred on the motor-way, and was ticked off by his elders and betters; there had been a punch-up outside the Odeon, but few sexual esca-pades this week—as far as the young ones were concerned—because of the weather.

"What about you, Tall Boy?" Dusty asked.

Jasper smiled and shrugged. "Well, I just had a quiet time," he said.

The birthday-card had not arrived that morning. At first, he had been disappointed, for the lack of it made his birthday seem not to have happened, but now he had begun to look forward to finding it there when he got home from work. He kept fingering the knot of his tie, and opening the collar of his overalls more.

"Hey, Tall Boy, what the devil you got there?" Buster came over, stared at Jasper's tie, then appeared to be blinded by it, reeling away theatrically, saying "Strewth!" his hands over his eyes.

Some of the others joined in in a wonderful, warm sort of abuse—just how they talked to one another, and which made Jasper so happy, grinning, putting up his fists at them, dancing up and down on his toes like a boxer.

"No, come off it, mate," Dusty said, recovering a little. "You can't wear that."

"It's hand-painted," said Jasper. "I got it for my birthday."

"So it's his birthday," Dusty said, turning to the others. He advanced slowly, menacingly towards Jasper, stuck out his finger and prodded his tie. "You know what that means, don't you?"

To prolong the delight of being in the middle of it all, Jasper pretended that he did not.

"It means," said Dusty slowly, knocking his fist against Jasper's chest. "It means, Tall Boy, you got to buy the cakes for tea."

"Yeah, that's right," said Buster. "You buy the cakes."

"I know, I know," said Jasper in his sing-song voice. He threw back his head and gave his high bubbling laugh, and jingled coins in both his pockets.

The weather had brightened and, as Jasper walked home from work, groups of women were sitting out on the steps of houses, waiting for their husbands to come home, shouting warnings to their children playing on the pavements.

Traffic at this hour was heavy and the streets were crowded, as London was emptying out its workers— thousands of arteries drawing them away, farther and farther from the heart of the city, out to the edges of the countryside.

At home, his birthday-card was waiting for him, and there was a miracle there, too; something he hardly dared to pick up—one of the rare letters from home, come on the right day. He sat down on the edge of the bed and opened it. Mam could never write much. It was a great labour and impatience to her to put pen to paper, and here was only a line or two to say the money had arrived safely and all were well. She did not mention his birthday. When she was writing, it must have been far ahead, and out of mind.

The letter was folded round a photograph. Who had taken it, he could not imagine; but there were the three little girls, his sisters, sitting on the steps of the wooden house—Opal, Crystal and Sapphyra. They were grinning straight at him, and Sapphyra's middle top teeth were missing. She looked quite different, he thought for a moment; then decided no, she was the same—the lovely same. He stared at the photograph for a long time, then got up with a jerk, and put it on the shelf by his bed, propped against the alarm clock, and his birthday-card beside it.

He went to the window and pushed down the sash and leaned out, his elbows resting on the frame. The noise of children playing came up. He had a peaceful feeling, listening to the street sounds, looking at a golden, dying light on the rooftops across the road.

He stayed there until the gold went out of the light, and he felt suddenly hungry. Then he shut the window, un-hooked the frying-pan and took an opener to a tin of beans. He smiled as he edged the opener round the rim. "They liked the cakes," he kept on thinking. The cakes he'd bought for tea.

He squatted by the gas-ring, turning the beans about

in the pan, humming to himself. He was glad he'd bought the tie—otherwise they'd never have known, and he could never have treated them. The tie had been a good idea. He might give it another airing, this nice, dry evening—stroll among the crowds outside the Odeon and the bowling alley.

He ate the beans out of the pan, spooning them up contentedly as he sat on the bed, staring at Opal and Crystal and Sapphyra, who grinned cheekily back at him, sitting in a neat row, their bare feet stuck out in front of them, out of focus, and sharp black shadows falling on their white dresses.

Praises

THE sunlight came through dusty windows into Miss
Smythe's Gown Department on the first floor of the
building. Across the glass were red and white notices
announcing the clearance sale. It was an early summer's
early evening, and the London rush hour at its worst. Rush
hours were now over for Miss Smythe, and she listened
to the hum of this one, feeling strange not to be stepping along the crowded pavement towards the Underground.

In a corner of the department some of the juniors had
begun to blow up balloons. The last customers had gone,
and several of the office staff came in with trays of glasses.
With remarkable deftness as soon as the shop was closed—
for the last time—they had draped and decorated Miss
Smythe's display counter, and they set the trays down on
this.

The great store, built in the 1860s, was due for demo-
lition. As business had slowly failed, like a tide on its way
out, the value of the site had gone on growing. The building had lately seemed to be demolishing itself, or at least
not hindering its happening. Its green dome still stood
with acid clarity against the summer sky; but the stone
walls had not been washed for many years and were black
with grime and dashed by pigeons' droppings.

The red and white SALE notices added to the look of
dereliction. In the past, sales had been discreetly managed,
really not more than a passing round of the word. The

77

clientele—the ex-clientele—was miserable about the notices. Going by in Bentleys and taxis, they glanced away, hurt, as if catching an old friend out in some vulgarity.

Miss Smythe trod softly across the carpeted way to the ladies' cloakroom—the customers' cloakroom. Here she took off her rings—her mother's engagement ring and her father's signet—and carefully washed her hands. She went over and over with the lather, as if she were about to perform an operation. Then she took a long time drying her hands, easing back cuticles, from habit, and looking thoughtfully about her.

She passed a hand over grey, tightly-permed hair, and studied herself in the full-length glass. She knew that a presentation was to be made, and she wished to look her best. It was rumoured that Mr Wakelin himself was to give a little speech.

Her figure was more imposing by being top-heavy. Although her hips were quite trim and her legs slender— she prided herself on her legs—her bosom was full, and there was a softness about her sloping shoulders. Her hands were plump, too, and white. She also prided herself on her hands.

Back in the salon things were livening up, and assistants from other departments crowding in. She saw her friend, Miss Fortescue, from Hats. (Millinery was not a word one used: clients who did were subtly put right.) Miss Fortescue, a younger woman than Miss Smythe, now had to find another position. It would not be easy for her, in her forties. However, she had a gentleman friend and could marry tomorrow if she cared to, as she had often told her juniors.

Miss Smythe did not discuss her private life with her assistants. Some mornings she had arrived with a bunch of flowers, and let the girls conjecture. There was really nothing to conjecture. She had lived alone since her parents died and knew that she always would, being now too fastidious, she thought, for marriage.

She was glad that it was time for her to retire. She could not have brought herself to work elsewhere, or to lower her standards. She had grown old along with her customers. Some she had known as young women, brought by their mothers to the salon for the first time. In those days she had been an assistant, handing pins and running errands. In these last years, or perhaps it was since the war, young women had not come with their mothers. Miss Smythe always enquired after them, but never met them.

"Well, you'll be glad to see the back of it all," Miss Fortescue said to her. "These last few weeks!"

"It has had its sordid side," Miss Smythe agreed. "But, no, I shan't be glad to see the back of it."

Some of the last marked-down, soiled, leftover garments lay crumpled on countertops, as if at a jumble sale, and, really, Miss Fortescue complained, some of the goods she had been expected to dispose of had come from a by-gone age. "We now know what 'old hat' means," she had told her assistants, spinning round on her hand a confection of satin and osprey feathers. She *was* too familiar with the girls, and they led her on with a kind of sycophantic raillery, even daring.

79

The evening sun slanted across the room at its last angle, showing up shabbiness. Where fixtures and show-cases had already been removed the surrounding walls had dirty, yellowing paint, and there were cobwebs cling-ing to nails. For days the cleaners—those who remained—had done nothing but shift stock. In this showroom the trodden carpet, once so deep, so rich, had been left, and the dusty chandelier with its grubby drops of glass, its rosettes and flutings. Someone, giggling, climbed on to a stool and tied a bunch of balloons to it.

One of Miss Smythe's own girls came to her with a tray of drinks and she put out her plump white hand and selected a glass of sherry. She also accepted from someone else two prawns on a little biscuit. Soon there would be crumbs and cigarette ash all over her carpet; but it was gritty already, with days of people traipsing through. She remembered it when it was new, replacing the faded moss-green one of her early days, and of how proud she was of it, for it was her own, she alone had been responsible for it. Now she watched ash being flicked on it—regardless, as she told herself.

Because her showroom had been chosen for the party, Miss Smythe was regarded as their hostess by the older members of the staff. They came to greet her as soon as they entered—old Mr Messenger from Accounts, the Restaurant manageress, and Miss Chivers from Hairdressing.

She received them graciously, standing beneath the decorated chandelier; but was not too much taken up with them to ignore one of her own girls who, drinking her third gin-and-French, was laughing noisily. She gave her one of her little glances and, for the first time, the girl looked at her defiantly, as if to imply that the old reign was over; habit won, however, and she fell silent.

"My dear Miss Smythe," said Mr Wakelin, coming in almost unnoticed, taking her hand. He was an unknown figure to most of those present, who were ruled by his underlings and hardly wondered if there were anyone in higher authority.

Miss Smythe received him with her usual poise. She had served royalty in her time, and knew how to behave—with calm deference, but her own kind of dignity.

Ineffectually Mr Wakelin tapped with a gold pencil on the side of his glass; then someone helpfully—but without taste, Miss Smythe thought—banged on a tray. "Un-called for," was always one of her sternest terms of condemnation.

"This poignant party," Mr Wakelin began, standing beside her. She moved back a little, discreetly. "For it is farewell for all of us," he went on, "for some after many, many years."

Miss Smythe looked down at the carpet, saw a match-stick, but forbore to pick it up.

With great authority, Mr Wakelin handed his glass to someone standing nearby; unhurriedly took out his bifocal spectacles, polished them, put them on, took from his pocket a piece of paper. He glanced at this and touched the knot of his Old Etonian tie. No one moved. Ah! the *savoir faire*! Miss Smythe thought admiringly.

"Our dear old friend, Mr Messenger, from Accounts," Mr Wakelin said. He smiled across at him and made a little joke about his resistance to the computer being installed, and a ruffle of laughter came from his staff, and then clapping as he came forward to accept an envelope and a gold watch, handed first to Mr Wakelin by his secretary. Besides their envelopes Miss Fortescue received a tooled leather writing case, the Restaurant manageress a fountain pen. It was obvious that Mr Wakelin's secretary had known how to grade the presents.

"And to all of you—some of you for too short a time our friends—I say thank you for your loyalty and support, and not least in these last difficult weeks; and may God go with you in all your days, and bring you into your desired haven."

A deeply religious man, Miss Smythe had always heard, and his beautiful, unhurried voice and the last cadence brought tears into her eyes. All the same, she was a little shocked, a little embarrassed, thinking he had finished speaking. Someone even began to clap. However, raising his hand and turning towards her he went on: "I have left mention of Miss Smythe until the very end." For a moment she had been afraid that his secretary had at last been found wanting, but there she was at his side, with the last parcel and envelope.

Because of her momentary confusion, Mr Wakelin's words came as a shock to Miss Smythe, sweeping away her emotion, making her feel apprehensive.

"How long Miss Smythe has been with us is her own secret," Mr Wakelin said. "I will only say that she is our oldest friend, and one who has never faltered, never failed us. Never spared herself, or lowered the standards which so many young people under her have learned to accept and live by. This is no mean thing to look back upon, at the end of a successful career, and I hope that she will do so with pleasure and satisfaction in many years of happy retirement.

"Much of the good that has been done in this . . . well, I almost said *hallowed* building . . . can be traced to her influence. And nothing that was wrong *can* be. The building will go, alas! as you all know; but that spirit will be scattered more broadly because of it. So out of disaster comes good; out of sorrow, inspiration. Miss Smythe, this present which I give you on behalf of the company and your colleagues cannot be in any measure what you deserve, but simply a token of our respect and, may I say, our love? Under this roof, where you have served so long, I should like to think that the last words said were yours."

Miss Smythe stepped forward and took the little gift-wrapped, oblong box. She stood under the chandelier again, holding her present in both hands before her, and thanked them all, after half-turning to Mr Wakelin to thank him personally.

His rhythm was infectious, and she fell easily into it.

"I shall not say very much to you," she continued, "for there is so little to be said. Our hearts have their own knowledge, and there we must strive to keep alive all that went on here—even when we see another building standing where this one stood, and others working in it.

"It has been a great thing to all of us, I know; but may I for a moment be personal? For this place has been my life." (One of her juniors thought it strange that the word 'shop' had not been mentioned all evening.) "And I have never wanted another. I remember the great days. It has been my privilege to serve—and to have for friends—the highest in the land. It has been a—a very glamorous life."

She stepped back, and the clapping began again. Mr Wakelin thanked her quietly, obviously much moved, conversation broke out and the trays were being carried round.

Five minutes after Mr Wakelin left, Miss Smythe decided, was her time to go. She did her rounds, put on her Persian lamb coat and her paisley turban and went down in the lift for the last time.

The street had a golden, dusty look; there were flowers on barrows, and the smell of them in the air. The rush hour was over.

She repeated in her mind, as she went towards the Underground, the words of Mr Wakelin's speech. So many had flown away for ever, but a few phrases she captured and imprisoned. All the way to Marylebone station she was in a strange state, as if the two glasses of sherry had gone to her head.

It was an unfamiliar train she got into, and none of her regular friends was on it—all gone homewards long ago. Strangers got in and sat in silence. In one day her friends had vanished. And those years of coming on the train from Denham had made many friends for her—even gentlemen friends, the only ones of that kind she had ever had. "Good morning, Miss Smythe, and how are we this morning? Now, can you help me with nine across? Animal wrongly chained. Seven letters, h the third."

After a while of looking at her own *Daily Telegraph*, she could say 'Echidna', and blush at her erudition.

"Miss Smythe, you are a genius." Perhaps, she thought, she had had too much praise all her life, and nothing else. Or might have been praised so much, *because* she had nothing else.

And her train friends, even if not—all of them— gentlemen, had been so gentlemanly. Mr Parkinson, so gallant; Mr Taylor, so serious-minded; Mr Westropp, that great rose-grower, a little flirtatious, but nothing objectionable—leaning out of the carriage window, lifting his folded *Times* to signal to her as she came on to the platform. "We can't take off without Miss Smythe."

And sometimes he brought those bouquets of roses from his garden in Gerrards Cross over which the juniors —Miss Smythe's girls—had conjectured; or, much earlier in the year, bunches of what he called 'daffs'. He was well-intentioned and Miss Smythe, deploring 'daffs', forgave him although none of her clients, for whom she took her standards, would have allowed the word (or non-word) to pass their lips.

Now she opened her large handbag and looked at the beautifully wrapped package. She knew what it was and had one already, but would treasure it none the less. She would have liked to have shown it to Mr Parkinson and the others, but would probably never see them again.

Too much praise? She wondered again. But it would have to last her for the rest of her life, and she had to remember it. She wished that she had refused the second glass of sherry, for her head ached and she kept recalling a jarring note amongst the praises.

When she had told them of her glamorous life, one of the women from the alterations room had smothered a laugh—or pretended to try to smother it. For Miss Smythe had had her battles. It had not been, all of it, a bed of roses without thorns. *That* woman had been a thorn. A *thorn*, Miss Smythe repeated to herself, glancing muzzily out at fleeting houses and gardens.

There had been, lately, enemies up there in the alteration room. That one especially. The chief thorn, kneeling in the fitting room, going round a hemline, flicking pins out of the black velvet pad on her wrist, spitting out measurements. For she resented criticism. And workmanship was a thing of the past, of the days of shoulder-paddings and moulded bustlines. Now they had nothing to do but take up a straight skirt an inch.

The Persian lamb was too warm for this evening; but she wore it because she had it. And it was the slowest journey she had ever made along that line—stopping at every station. Coming out of London in this sunset, on this last day, everything looked new to her—she noted men working in blossoming gardens, stretches of water with sea-gulls on them, and silver birches, her favourite tree.

The stations at which they stopped were like sets in an old Western film, ramshackle with wooden buildings, and pointed slat fences and platform shelters. And no one about. No streams of dark-suited men hastening, with their evening papers, towards the ticket barriers.

She sat back idly, her hands clasped over the bag on her lap, and looked out of the window at the evening scene as if for the first time, not the last.

In and Out the Houses

KITTY Miller, wearing a new red hair-ribbon, bounced along the Vicarage drive, skipping across ruts
and jumping over puddles.

Visiting took up all of her mornings in the school
holidays. From kitchen to kitchen, round the village, she
made her progress, and, this morning, felt drawn towards
the Vicarage. Quite sure of her welcome, she tapped on the
back door.

"Why, Kitty Miller!" said the Vicar, opening it. He
looked quite different from in church Kitty thought. He
was wearing an open-necked shirt and an old, darned
cardigan. He held a tea-towel to the door-handle, because
his fingers were sticky. He and his wife were cutting up
Seville oranges for marmalade and there was a delicious,
tangy smell about the kitchen.

Kitty took off her coat, and hung it on the usual peg,
and fetched a knife from the dresser drawer.

"You are on your rounds again," Mr Edwards said.
"Spreading light and succour about the parish."

Kitty glanced at him rather warily. She preferred him
not to be there, disliking men about her kitchens. She
reached for an orange, and watching Mrs Edwards for
a moment out of the corners of her eyes, began to slice
it up.

"What's new?" asked the Vicar.

"Mrs Saddler's bad," she said accusingly. He should be
at that bedside, she meant to imply, instead of making

marmalade. "They were staying at The Horse and Groom that she won't last the day."

"So we are not your first call of the morning?"

She had, on her way here, slipped round the back of the pub and into the still-room, where Miss Betty Benford, eight months pregnant, was washing the floor, puffing and blowing as she splashed grey soapy water over the flags with a gritty rag. When this job was done—to Miss Betty's mind, not Kitty's—they drank a cup of tea together and chatted about the baby, woman to woman. The village was short of babies, and Kitty visualised pushing this one out in its pram, taking it round with her on her visits.

In his office, the landlord had been typing the luncheon menus. The keys went down heavily, his finger hovered, and stabbed. He often made mistakes, and this morning had typed 'Jam Fart and Custard'. Kitty considered— and then decided against—telling the Vicar this.

"They have steak-and-kidney pie on the set menu to-day," she said instead.

"My favourite!" groaned the Vicar. "I *never* get it."

"You had it less than a fortnight ago," his wife reminded him.

"And what pudding? If it's treacle tart I shall cry bitterly."

"Jam tart," Kitty said gravely. "And custard."

"I quite like custard, too," he said simply.

"Or choice of cheese and biscuits."

"I should have cheese and biscuits," Mrs Edwards said.

It was just the kind of conversation Kitty loved.

"Eight-and-sixpence," she said. "Coffee extra."

"To be rich! To be rich!" The Vicar said. "And what are *we* having, my dear? Kitty has caused the juices to run."

"Cold, of course, as it's Monday."

He shuddered theatrically, and picked up another orange. "My day off, too!"

Kitty pressed her lips together primly, thinking it wrong for clergymen to have days off, especially with Mrs Saddler lying there, dying.

The three of them kept glancing at one another's work as they cut the oranges. Who was doing it finely enough? Only Mrs Edwards, they all knew.

"I like it fairly chunky," the Vicar said.

When it was all done, Kitty rinsed her hands at the sink, and then put on her coat. She had given the Vicarage what time she could spare, and the morning was getting on, and all the rest of the village waiting. She was very orderly in her habits and never visited in the afternoons, for then she had her novel to write. The novel was known about in the village, and some people felt concerned, wondering if she might be another little Daisy Ashford.

With the Vicar's phrases of gratitude giving her momentum, Kitty tacked down the drive between the shabby laurels, and out into the lane.

"The Vicar's having cold," she told Mrs De Vries, who was preparing a *tajine* of chicken in a curious earthenware pot she had brought back from Morocco.

"Poor old Vicar," Mrs De Vries said absent-mindedly, as she cut almonds into slivers. She had a glass of something on the draining-board and often took a sip from it. "Do run and find a drink for yourself, dear child," she said. She was one of the people who wondered about Daisy Ashford.

"I'll have a bitter lemon, if I may," Kitty said.

"Well, do, my dear. You know where to find it."

As Kitty knew everything about nearly every house in the village, she did not reply; but went with assurance to the bar in the hall. She stuck a plastic straw in her drink, and returned to the kitchen sucking peacefully.

"Is there anything I can do?" she enquired.

"No, just tell me the news. What's going on?"

"Mr Mumford typed 'Jam Fart and Custard' on the menu card."

"Oh, he didn't! You've made me do the nose-trick with my gin. The *pain* of it!" Mrs De Vries snatched a handkerchief from her apron pocket and held it to her face. When she had recovered, she said, "I simply can't wait for Tom to come home, to tell him that."

Kitty looked modestly gratified. "I called at the Vicarage, too, on my way."

"And what were *they* up to?"

"They are up to making marmalade."

"Poor darlings! They *do* have to scrimp and scratch. Church mice, indeed!"

"But isn't home-made marmalade nicer than shop?"

"Not all *that* much."

After a pause, Kitty said, "Mrs Saddler's on her way out."

"Who the hell's Mrs Saddler?"

"At the almshouse. She's dying."

"Poor old thing."

Kitty sat down on a stool and swung her fat legs.

"Betty Benford is eight months gone," she said shrugging her shoulders.

"I wish you'd tell me something about people I *know*," Mrs De Vries complained, taking another sip of gin.

"Her mother plans to look after the baby while Betty goes on going out to work. Mrs Benford, you know."

"Not next door's daily?"

"She won't be after this month."

"Does Mrs Glazier know?" Mrs De Vries asked, inclining her head towards next door.

"Not yet," Kitty said, glancing at the clock.

"My God, she'll go up the wall," Mrs De Vries said with relish. "She's had that old Benford for years and years."

"What do you call that you're cooking?"

"It's a *tajine* of chicken."

"Mrs De Vries is having *tajine* of chicken," Kitty said next door five minutes later.

"And what might that be when it's at home?"

Kitty described it as best she could, and Mrs Glazier looked huffy. "Derek wouldn't touch it," she said. "He likes good, plain, English food, and no messing about."

She was rolling out pastry for that evening's steak-and-kidney pie.

"They're having that at The Horse and Groom," Kitty said.

"*And* we'll have sprouts. *And* braised celery," Mrs Glazier added, not letting Mrs De Vries get away with her airs and graces.

"Shall I make a pastry rose to go on the top of the pie?" Kitty offered. "Mrs Prout showed me how to."

"No, I think we'll leave well alone."

"Do you like cooking?" Kitty asked in a conversational tone.

"I don't mind it. Why?"

"I was only thinking that then it wouldn't be so hard on you when Mrs Benford leaves."

Mrs Benford was upstairs. There was a bumping, droning noise of a vacuum cleaner above, in what Kitty knew to be Mrs Glazier's bedroom.

Mrs Glazier, with an awful fear in her heart, stared, frowning, at Kitty, who went on, "I was just telling Mrs De Vries that after Mrs Benford's grandchild's born she's going to stay at home to mind it."

The fact that next door had heard this stunning news first made the blow worse, and Mrs Glazier put a flour-covered hand to her forehead. She closed her eyes for a moment. "But why can't the girl look after the little— baby herself?"

Kitty took the lid off a jar marked 'Cloves' and looked inside, sniffing. "Her daughter earns more money at The Horse and Groom than her mother earns here," she explained.

"I suppose you told Mrs De Vries that too."

Kitty went to the door with dignity. "Oh, no! I never talk from house to house. My mother says I'll have to stop my visiting, if I do. Oh, by the way," she called back,

"You'd better keep your dog in. The De Vries's bitch is on heat."

She went home and sat down to lamb and bubble-and-squeak.

"The Vicar's having cold, too," she said.

"And that's *his* business," her mother said warningly.

A few days later, Kitty called on Mrs Prout.

Mrs Prout's cottage was one of Kitty's favourite visits. Many years ago, before she was married, Mrs Prout had been a school-teacher, and she enjoyed using her old skills to deal with Kitty. Keeping her patience pliant, she taught her visitor new card games (and they were all educational), and got her on to collecting and pressing wild-flowers. She would give her pastry-trimmings to cut into shapes, and showed her how to pop corn and make fudge. She was extremely kind, though firm, and Kitty respected the rules —about taking off her Wellingtons and washing her hands and never calling on Mondays or Thursdays, because these were turning-out days when Mrs Prout was far too busy to have company.

They were very serious together. Mrs Prout enjoyed being authoritative to a child again, and Kitty had a sense of orderliness which obliged her to comply.

"They sent this from the Vicarage," she said, coming into the kitchen with a small pot of marmalade.

"How jolly nice!" Mrs Prout said. She took the marmalade, and tilted it slightly, and it moved. Rather sloppy. But she thought no worse of the Vicar's wife for that.

"That's really *jolly* nice of them," she said, going into the larder. "And they shall have some of my apple jelly, in fair return. *Quid pro quo*, eh? And one good turn deserves another."

She came out of the larder with a different little pot and held it to the light; but the clear and golden content did not move when she tipped it sideways.

"What's the news?" she asked.

"Mrs Saddler still lingers on," Kitty said. She had called at the almshouse to enquire, but the district nurse had told her to run off and mind her own business. "I looked in at the Wilsons' on my way here. Mrs Wilson was making a cheese and onion pie. Of course, they're vegetarians; but I have known him to sneak a little chicken into his mouth. I was helping to hand round at the De Vries's cocktail-party, and he put out his hand towards a patty. 'It's chicken,' I said to him in a low voice. 'Nary a word,' he said, and he winked at me and ate it."

"And now you *have* said a word," Mrs Prout said briskly.

"Why, so I have," Kitty agreed, looking astonished.

Mrs Prout cleared the kitchen table in the same brisk way, and said, "If you like, now, I'll show you how to make ravioli. We shall have it for our television supper."

"Make ravioli," cried Kitty. "You can't *make* ravioli. Mrs Glazier buys it in a tin."

"So Mrs Glazier may. But I find time to make my own."

"I shall be fascinated," Kitty said, taking off her coat.

"Then wash your hands, and don't forget to dry them properly. Isn't it about time you cut your nails?" Mrs Prout asked, in her school-mistressy voice, and Kitty, who would take anything from her, agreed. ("We all know Mrs Prout is God," her mother sometimes said resentfully.)

"Roll up those sleeves, now. And we'll go through your tables while we work."

Mrs Prout set out the flour bin and a dredger and a pastry-cutter and the mincer. Going back and forth to the cupboard, she thought how petty she was to be pleased at knowing that by this time tomorrow, most of the village would be aware that she made her own ravioli. But perhaps it was only human, she decided.

"Now this is what chefs call the *mise en place*," she explained to Kitty, when she had finished arranging the table. "Can you remember that? *Mise en place*."

"*Mise en place*," Kitty repeated obediently.

"Shall I help you prepare the *mise en place*?" Kitty enquired of Mrs Glazier.

"Mr Glazier wouldn't touch it. I've told you he will only eat English food."

"But you have ravioli. That's Italian."

"I just keep it as a stand-by," Mrs Glazier said scornfully. She was very huffy and put out these days, especially with Mrs De Vries next door and her getting the better of her every time. Annette de Vries was French, and didn't they all know it. Mrs Glazier, as a result, had become violently insular.

"I can make ravioli," Kitty said, letting the *mise en place* go, for she was not absolutely certain about it. "Mrs Prout has just been teaching me. She and Mr Prout have television trays by the fire, and then they sit and crack walnuts and play cards, and then they have hot milk and whisky and go to bed. I think it is very nice and cosy, don't you?"

"Mr Glazier likes a proper sit-down meal when *he* gets back. Did you happen to see Tiger anywhere down the lane?"

"No, but I expect he's next door. I told you their bitch is on heat. You ought to shut him up."

"It's their affair to shut *theirs* up."

"Well, I'm just calling there, so I'll shoo him off."

She had decided to cut short this visit. Mrs Glazier was so bad-tempered these days, and hardly put herself out at all to give a welcome, and every interesting thing Kitty told her served merely to annoy.

"And I must get on with my jugged hare," Mrs Glazier said, making no attempt to delay the departure. "It should be marinating in the port wine by now," she added grandly. "And I must make the soup and the croutons."

"Well, then, I'll be going," Kitty said, edging towards the door.

"And apricot mousse," Mrs Glazier called out after her, as if she were in a frenzy.

"Shall I prepare your *mise en place?*" Kitty enquired of Mrs De Vries, trying her luck again.

"My! We *are* getting professional," said Mrs De Vries, but her mind was really on what Kitty had just been telling her. Soup and jugged hare! She was thinking. What a dreadful meal!

She was glazing a terrine of chicken livers and wished

that all the village might see her work of art, but having Kitty there was the next best thing.

"What's that?" she asked, as Kitty put the jar of apple jelly on the table.

"I have to take it to the Vicarage on my way home. It's some of Mrs Prout's apple jelly."

Mrs De Vries gave it a keen look, and notched up one point to Mrs Prout. She notched up another when she heard about the ravioli, and wondered if she had under-estimated the woman.

"I shooed that Tiger away," Kitty said.

"The wretched cur. He is driving Topaze insane."

Kitty mooched round the kitchen, peeking and prying. Mrs De Vries was the only one in the village to possess a *mandoline* for cutting vegetables. There was a giant pestle and mortar, a wicker bread-basket, ropes of Spanish onions, and a marble cheese-tray.

"You can pound the fish for me, if you have the energy," said Mrs De Vries.

As this was not a house where she was made to wash her hands first, Kitty immediately set to work.

"I was just going to have pears," Mrs De Vries said, in a half-humorous voice. "But if the Glaziers are going in for apricot mousse I had better pull my socks up. That remark, of course, is strictly *entre nous*."

"Then Mrs De Vries pulled her socks up, and made a big apple tart," Kitty told her mother.

"I have warned you before, Kitty. What you see going on in people's houses, you keep to yourself. Or you stay

98

out of them. Is that finally and completely under-stood?"

"Yes, Mother," Kitty said meekly.

"My dear girl, I couldn't eat it. I couldn't eat another thing," said Mr Glazier, confronted by the apricot mousse. "A three-course-meal. Why, I shouldn't sleep all night if I had any more. The hare alone was ample."

"I think Mr De Vries would do better justice to his dinner," said Mrs Glazier bitterly. She had spent all day cooking and was exhausted. "It's not much fun slaving away and not being appreciated. And what on earth can I do with all the left-overs?"

"Finish them up tomorrow and save yourself a lot of trouble."

Glumly, Mrs Glazier washed the dishes, and suddenly thought of the Prouts sitting peacefully beside their fire, cracking walnuts, playing cards. She felt ill-done-by, as she stacked the remains of dinner in the fridge, but was per-fectly certain that lie as she might have to to Kitty in the morning, the whole village should not know that for the second day running the Glaziers were having soup, and jugged hare, and apricot mousse.

Next day, eating a slice of apple tart, Kitty saw Mrs De Vries test the soup and then put the ladle back into the saucepan. "What the eye doesn't see, the heart cannot grieve over," Mrs De Vries said cheerfully. She added salt, and a turn or two of pepper. Then she took more than a sip from the glass on the draining-board, seeming to find it more to her liking than the soup.

"The Vicarage can't afford drinks," Kitty said.

"They *do* confide in you."

"I said to the Vicar, Mrs De Vries drinks gin while she is cooking, and he said, 'Lucky old her'."

"There will be a lot of red faces about this village if you go on like this," said Mrs De Vries, making her part of the prophecy come true at once. Kitty looked at her in surprise. Then she said—Mrs De Vries's flushed face reminding her —"I think next door must be having the change of life. She is awfully grumpy these days. Nothing pleases her."

"You are too knowing for your years," Mrs De Vries said, and she suddenly wished she had not been so un-hygienic about the soup. Too late now. "How is your novel coming along?" she enquired.

"Oh, very nicely, thank you. I expect I shall finish it before I go back to school, and then it can be published for Christmas."

"We shall all look forward to that," said Mrs De Vries, in what Kitty considered an unusual tone of voice.

"Mrs De Vries cuts up her vegetables with a *mandoline*," Kitty told Mrs Glazier some days later.

"I always knew she must be nuts," said Mrs Glazier, thinking of the musical instrument.

Seeing Kitty dancing up the drive, she had quickly hidden the remains of a shepherd's pie at the back of a cupboard. She was more than ever ruffled this morning, because Mrs Benford had not arrived or sent a message.

She had also been getting into a frenzy with her ravioli and, in the end, had thrown the whole lot into the dust-bin. She hated waste, especially now that her house-keeping allowance always seemed to have disappeared by Wednesday, and her husband was, in his dyspeptic way, continually accusing her of extravagance.

Kitty had been hanging about outside the almshouses for a great part of the morning, and had watched Mrs Saddler's coffin being carried across the road to the church.

"Only one wreath and two relations," she now told Mrs Glazier. "That's what comes of being poor. What are you having for dinner tonight? I could give you a hand."

"Mr Glazier will probably be taking me to the Horse and Groom for a change," Mrs Glazier lied.

"They are all at sixes and sevens there. Betty Benford started her pains in the night. A fortnight early. Though Mr Mumford thinks she may have made a mistake with her dates."

Then Mrs Benford would never come again, Mrs Glazier thought despondently. She had given a month's notice the week before, and Mrs Glazier had received it coldly, saying—"I think I should have been informed of this before it became common gossip in the village." Mrs Benford had seemed quite taken aback at that.

"Well, I mustn't hang around talking," Mrs Glazier told Kitty. "There's a lot to do this morning, and will be from now on. When do you go back to school?"

"On Thursday."

Mrs Glazier nodded, and Kitty felt herself dismissed. She sometimes wondered why she bothered to pay this call, when everyone else made her so welcome; but coming away from the funeral she had seen Mrs De Vries driving into town, and it was one of Mrs Prout's turning-out days. She had hardly liked to call at the Vicarage under the circumstances of the funeral, and The Horse and Groom being at sixes and sevens had made everyone there very boring and busy.

"I hope you will enjoy your dinner," she said politely to Mrs Glazier. "They have roast Surrey fowl and all the trimmings."

When she had gone, Mrs Glazier took the shepherd's pie from its hiding place, and began to scrape some shabby old carrots.

"Kitty, will you stop chattering and get on with your pudding," her mother said in an exasperated voice.

Kitty had been describing how skilfully the undertaker's men had lowered Mrs Saddler's coffin into the grave, Kitty herself peering from behind the tombstone of Maria Britannia Marlowe—her favourite dead person on account of her name.

It was painful to stop talking. A pain came in her chest, severe enough to slow her breathing, and gobbling the rice pudding made it worse. As soon as her plate was cleared she began again. "Mrs Glazier has the change of life," she said.

"How on earth do you know about such things?" her mother asked in a faint note.

"As *you* didn't tell me, I had to find out the hard way," Kitty said sternly.

Her mother pursed her lips together to stop laughing, and began to stack up the dishes.

"How Mrs De Vries will miss me!" Kitty said dreamily, rising to help her mother. "I shall be stuck there at school doing boring things, and she'll be having a nice time drinking gin."

"Now *that* is enough. You are to go to your room immediately," her mother said sharply, and Kitty looked at her red face reflectively, comparing it with Mrs Glazier's. "You will have to find some friends of your own age. You are becoming a little menace to everyone with your visiting, and we have got to live in this village. Now upstairs you go, and think over what I have said."

"Very well, mother," Kitty said meekly. If she did not have to help mother with the washing-up, she could get on with her novel all the sooner.

She went upstairs to her bedroom and spread her writing things out on the table and soon, having at once forgotten her mother's words, was lost in the joy of authorship.

Her book was all about little furry animals, and their small adventures, and there was not a human being in it, except the girl, Katherine, who befriended them all.

She managed a few more visits that holiday; but on Thursday she went back to school again, and then no one in the village knew what was happening any more.

Flesh

PHYL was always one of the first to come into the hotel bar in the evenings, for what she called her *aperitif*, and which, in reality, amounted to two hours' steady drinking. After that, she had little appetite for dinner, a meal to which she was not used.

On this evening, she had put on one of her beaded tops, of the kind she wore behind the bar on Saturday evenings in London, and patted back her tortoiseshell hair. She was massive and glittering and sunburnt—a wonderful sight, Stanley Archard thought, as she came across the bar towards him.

He had been sitting waiting for her. They had found their own level in one another on about the third day of the holiday. Both being heavy drinkers drew them together. Before that had happened, they had looked one another over warily as, in fact, they had all their fellow-guests.

Travelling on their own, speculating, both had watched and wondered. Even at the airport, she had stood out from the others, he remembered, as she had paced up and down in her emerald green coat. Then their flight number had been called, and they had gathered with others at the same channel, with the same pink labels tied to their hand luggage, all going to the same place; a polite, but distant little band of people, no one knowing with whom friendships were to be made—as like would no doubt drift to like. In the days that followed, Stanley had wished he had taken more notice of Phyl from the beginning, so that at the end of the holiday he would have that much more to remember. Only the emerald green coat had stayed in his mind. She had not worn it since—it was too warm—and he dreaded the day when she would put it on again to make the return journey.

Arriving in the bar this evening, she hoisted herself up on a stool beside him. "Well, here we are," she said, glowing, taking one peanut; adding, as she nibbled, "Evening, George," to the barman. "How's tricks?"

"My God, you've caught it today," Stanley said, and he put his hands up near her plump red shoulders as if to warm them at a fire. "Don't overdo it," he warned her.

"Oh, I never peel," she said airily.

He always put in a word against the sun-bathing when he could. It separated them. She stayed all day by the hotel swimming-pool, basting herself with oil. He, bored with basking—which made him feel dizzy—had hired a car and spent his time driving about the island, and was full of alienating information about the locality, which the other guests—resenting the hired car, too—did their best to avoid. Only Phyl did not mind listening to him. For nearly every evening of her married life she had stood behind the bar and listened to other people's boring chat: she had a technique for dealing with it and a fund of vague phrases. "Go on!" she said now, listening—hardly listening—to Stanley, and taking another nut. He had gone off by himself and found a place for lunch: *hors d'œuvre*, nice-sized slice of veal, two veg, *crème caramel*, half bottle of rosé, coffee—twenty-two shillings the lot.

"Well, I'm blowed," said Phyl, and she took a pound note from her handbag and waved it at the barman. When she snapped up the clasp of the bag it had a heavy, expensive sound.

One or two other guests came in and sat at the bar. At this stage of the holiday they were forming into little groups, and this was the jokey set who had come first after Stanley and Phyl. According to them all sorts of funny things had happened during the day, and little screams of laughter ran round the bar.

"Shows how wrong you can be," Phyl said in a low voice, "I thought they were ever so starchy on the plane. I was wrong about you, too. At the start, I thought you were . . . you know . . . one of *those*. Going about with that young boy all the time."

Stanley patted her knee. "On the contrary," he said, with a meaning glance at her. "No, I was just at a bit of a loose end, and he seemed to cotton on. Never been abroad before, he hadn't, and didn't know the routine. I liked it for the first day or two. It was like taking a nice kiddie out on a treat. Then it seemed to me he was sponging. I'm not mean, I don't think; but I don't like that—sponging. It was quite a relief when he suddenly took up with the Lisper."

By now, he and Phyl had nicknames for most of the other people in the hotel. They did not know that the same applied to them, and that to the jokey set he was known as Paws and she as the Shape. It would have put them out and perhaps ruined their holiday if they had known. He thought his little knee-pattings were of the utmost discretion, and she felt confidence from knowing her figure was expensively controlled under her beaded dresses when she became herself again in the evenings. During the day, while sun-bathing, she considered that anything went—that, as her mind was a blank, her body became one also.

The funny man of the party—the awaited climax—came into the bar, crabwise, face covered slyly with his hand, as if ashamed of some earlier misdemeanour. "Oh, my God, don't look round. Here comes trouble!" someone said loudly, and George was called for from all sides. "What's the poison, Harry? No, my shout, old boy. George, if you *please*."

Phyl smiled indulgently. It was just like Saturday night with the regulars at home. She watched George with a professional eye, and nodded approvingly. He was good. They could have used him at The Nelson. A good quick boy.

"Heard from your old man?" Stanley asked her.

She cast him a tragic, calculating look. "You must be joking. He can't *write*. No, honest, I've never had a letter from him in the whole of my life. Well, we always saw each other every day until I had my hysterectomy."

Until now, in conversations with Stanley, she had always referred to 'a little operation'. But he had guessed what it was—well, it always was, wasn't it?—and knew that it was the reason for her being on holiday. Charlie, her husband, had sent her off to recuperate. She had sworn there was no need, that she had never felt so well in her life —was only a bit weepy sometimes late on a Saturday night. "I'm not really the crying sort," she had explained to Stanley. "So he got worried, and sent me packing." "You clear off to the sun," he had said, "and see what that will do."

What the sun had done for her was to burn her brick-red, and offer her this nice holiday friend. Stanley Archard, retired widower from Hove.

She enjoyed herself, as she usually did. The sun shone every day, and the drinks were so reasonable—they had many a long discussion about that. They also talked about his little flat in Hove; his strolls along the front; his few cronies at the club; his sad, orderly and lonely life.

This evening, he wished he had not brought up the subject of Charlie's writing to her, for it seemed to have fixed her thoughts on him and, as she went chatting on about him, Stanley felt an indefinable distaste, an aloofness.

She brought out from her note-case a much-creased cutting from *The Morning Advertiser*. "Phyl and Charlie Parsons welcome old friends and new at The Nelson, Southwood. In licensed hours only!" "That was when we changed Houses," she explained. There was a photograph of them both standing behind the bar. He was wearing a dark blazer with a large badge on the pocket. Sequins gave off a smudged sparkle from her breast, her hair was newly, elaborately done, and her large, ringed hand rested on an ornamental beer-handle. Charlie had *his* hands in the blazer pockets, as if he were there to do the welcoming, and his wife to do the work: and this, in fact, was how things were. Stanley guessed it, and felt a twist of annoyance in his chest. He did not like the look of Charlie, or anything he had heard about him—how, for instance, he had seemed like a fish out of water visiting his wife in hospital. "He used to sit on the edge of the chair and stare at the clock, like a boy in school," Phyl had said, laughing. Stanley could not bring himself to laugh, too. He had leaned forward and taken her knee in his hand and wobbled it sympathetically to and fro.

No, she wasn't the crying sort, he agreed. She had a wonderful buoyancy and gallantry, and she seemed to knock years off his age by just *being* with him, talking to him.

In spite of their growing friendship, they kept to their original, separate tables in the hotel restaurant. It seemed too suddenly decisive and public a move for him to join her now, and he was too shy to carry it off at this stage of the holiday, before such an alarming audience. But after dinner, they would go for a walk along the sea-front, or out in the car for a drink at another hotel.

Always, for the first minute or two in a bar, he seemed to lose her. As if she had forgotten him, she would look about her critically, judging the set-up, sternly drawing attention to a sticky ring on the counter where she wanted to rest her elbow, keeping a professional eye on the prices.

When they were what she called 'nicely grinned-up', they liked to drive out to a small headland and park the car, watching the swinging beam from a lighthouse. Then, after the usual knee-pattings and neck-strokings, they would heave and flop about in the confines of the Triumph Herald, trying to make love. Warmed by their drinks, and the still evening and the romantic sound of the sea idly turning over down below them, they became frustrated, both large, solid people, she much corseted and, anyhow, beginning to be painfully sunburnt across the shoulders, he with the confounded steering-wheel to contend with.

He would grumble about the car and suggest getting out onto a patch of dry barley grass; but she imagined it full of insects; the chirping of the cicadas was almost deafening.

She also had a few scruples about Charlie, but they were not so insistent as the cicadas. After all, she thought, she had never had a holiday-romance—not even a honeymoon with Charlie—and she felt that life owed her just one.

After a time, during the day, her sunburn forced her into the shade, or out in the car with Stanley. Across her shoulders she began to peel, and could not bear—though desiring his caress—him to touch her. Rather glumly, he waited for her flesh to heal, told her 'I told you so'; after all, they had not forever on this island, had started their second, their last week already.

"I'd like to have a look at the other island," she said, watching the ferry leaving, as they sat drinking nearby.

"It's not worth just going there for the inside of a day," he said meaningfully, although it was only a short distance.

Wasn't this, both suddenly wondered, the answer to the too small car, and the watchful eyes back at the hotel. She had refused to allow him into her room there. "If anyone saw you going in or out. Why, they know where I live. What's to stop one of them coming into The Nelson any time, and chatting Charlie up?"

"Would you?" he now asked, watching the ferry starting off across the water. He hardly dared to hear her answer.

After a pause, she laughed. "Why not?" she said, and

took his hand. "We wouldn't really be doing any harm to anyone." (Meaning Charlie.) "Because no one could find out, could they?"

"Not over there," he said, nodding towards the island. "We can start fresh over there. Different people."

"They'll notice we're both not at dinner at the hotel."

"That doesn't prove anything."

She imagined the unknown island, the warm and starlit night and, somewhere, under some roof or other, a large bed in which they could pursue their daring, more than middle-aged adventure, unconfined in every way.

"As soon as my sunburn's better," she promised. "We've got five more days yet, and I'll keep in the shade till then."

A chambermaid advised yoghourt, and she spread it over her back and shoulders as best she could, and felt its coolness absorbing the heat from her skin.

Damp and cheesy-smelling in the hot night, she lay awake, cross with herself. For the sake of a tan, she was wasting her holiday—just to be a five minutes' wonder in the bar on her return, the deepest brown any of them had had that year. The darker she was, the more *abroad* she would seem to have been, the more prestige she could command. All summer, pallid herself, she had had to admire others.

Childish, really, she decided, lying rigid under the sheet, afraid to move, burning and throbbing. The skin was taut behind her knees, so that she could not stretch her legs; her flesh was on fire.

Five more days, she kept thinking. Meanwhile, even this sheet upon her was unendurable.

On the next evening, to establish the fact that they would not always be in to dinner at the hotel, they complained in the bar about the dullness of the menu, and went elsewhere.

It was a drab little restaurant, but they scarcely noticed their surroundings. They sat opposite one another at a corner table and ate shellfish briskly, busily—he, from his enjoyment of the food; she, with a wish to be rid of it. They rinsed their fingers, quickly dried them and leaned forward and twined them together—their large placid hands, with heavy rings, clasped on the tablecloth. Phyl, glancing aside for a moment, saw a young girl, at the next table with a boy, draw in her cheekbones to suppress laughter then, failing, turn her head to hide it.

"At *our* age," Phyl said gently, drawing away her hands from his. "In public, too."

She could not be defiant; but Stanley said jauntily, "I'm damned if I care."

At that moment, their chicken was placed before them, and he sat back, looking at it, waiting for vegetables.

As well as the sunburn, the heat seemed to have affected Phyl's stomach. She felt queasy and nervy. It was now their last day but one before they went over to the other island. The yoghourt—or time—had taken the pain from her back and shoulders, though leaving her with a dappled, flaky look, which would hardly bring forth cries of admiration or advance her prestige in the bar when she returned. But, no doubt, she thought, by then England would be too cold for her to go sleeveless. Perhaps the trees would have changed colour. She imagined—already—dark Sunday afternoons, their three o'clock lunch done with, and she and Charlie sitting by the electric log fire in a lovely hot room smelling of oranges and the so-called hearth littered with peel. Charlie—bless him—always dropped off amongst a confusion of newspapers, worn out with banter and light ale, switched off, too, as he always was with her, knowing that he could relax—be nothing, rather —until seven o'clock, because it was Sunday. Again, for Phyl, imagining home, a little pang, soon swept aside or, rather, swept aside *from*.

She was in a way relieved that they would have only one night on the little island. That would make it seem more like a chance escapade than an affair, something less serious and deliberate in her mind. Thinking about it during the day-time, she even felt a little apprehensive; but told herself sensibly that there was really nothing to worry about: knowing herself well, she could remind herself that an evening's drinking would blur all the nervous edges.

"I can't get over that less than a fortnight ago I never knew you existed," she said, as they drove to the afternoon ferry. "And after this week," she added, "I don't suppose I'll ever see you again."

"I wish you wouldn't talk like that—spoiling things,"

he said heavily, and he tried not to think of Hove, and the winter walks along the promenade, and going back to the flat, boiling himself a couple of eggs, perhaps; so desperately lost without Ethel.

He had told Phyl about his wife and their quiet happiness together for many years, and then her long, long illness, during which she seemed to be going away from him gradually; but it was dreadful all the same when she finally did.

"We could meet in London on your day off," he suggested.

"Well, maybe." She patted his hand, leaving that disappointment aside for him.

There were only a few people on the ferry. It was the end of summer, and the tourists were dwindling, as the English community was reassembling, after trips 'back home'.

The sea was intensely blue all the way across to the island. They stood by the rail looking down at it, marvelling, and feeling like two people in a film. They thought they saw a dolphin, which added to their delight.

"Ethel and I went to Jersey for our honeymoon," Stanley said. "It poured with rain nearly all the time, and Ethel had one of her migraines."

"I never had a honeymoon," Phyl said. "Just the one night at the Regent Palace. In our business, you can't both go away together. This is the first time I've ever been abroad."

"The places I could take you to," he said.

They drove the car off the ferry and began to cross the island. It was hot and dusty, hillsides terraced and tilled; green lemons hung on the trees.

"I wouldn't half like to actually *pick* a lemon," she said.

"You shall," he said, "somehow or other."

"And take it home with me," she added. She would save it for a while, showing people, then cut it up for gin and tonic in the bar one evening, saying casually, "I picked this lemon with my own fair hands."

Stanley had booked their hotel from a restaurant, on the recommendation of a barman. When they found it, he was openly disappointed; but she managed to be gallant and optimistic. It was not by the sea, with a balcony where they might look out at the moonlit waters or rediscover brightness in the morning; but down a dull side street, and opposite a garage.

"We don't *have* to," Stanley said doubtfully.

"Oh, come on! We might not get in anywhere else. It's only for sleeping in," she said.

"It *isn't* only for sleeping in," he reminded her.

An enormous man in white shirt and shorts came out to greet them. "My name is Radam. Welcome," he said, with confidence. "I have a lovely room for you, Mr and Mrs Archard. You will be happy here, I can assure you. My wife will carry up your cases. Do not protest, Mr Archard. She is quite able to. Our staff has slackened off at the end of the season, and I have some trouble with the old ticker, as you say in England. I know England well. I am a Bachelor of Science of England University. Once had digs in Swindon."

A pregnant woman shot out of the hotel porch and seized their suitcases, and there was a tussle as Stanley wrenched them from her hands. Still serenely boasting,

Mr Radam led them upstairs, all of them panting but himself.

The bedroom was large and dusty and overlooked a garage.

"Oh, God, I'm sorry," Stanley said, when they were left alone. "It's still not too late, if you could stand a row."

"No. I think it's rather sweet," Phyl said, looking round the room. "And, after all, don't blame yourself. You couldn't know any more than me."

The furniture was extraordinarily fret-worked, as if to make more crevices for the dust to settle in; the bedside-lamp base was an old gin bottle filled with gravel to weight it down, and when Phyl pulled off the bed cover to feel the bed she collapsed with laughter, for the pillow-cases were embroidered 'Hers' and 'Hers'.

Her laughter eased him, as it always did. For a moment, he thought disloyally of the dead—of how Ethel would have started to be depressed by it all, and he would have hard work jollying her out of her dark mood. At the same time, Phyl was wryly imagining Charlie's wrath, how he would have carried on—for only the best was good enough for him, as he never tired of saying.

"He's quite right—that awful fat man," she said gaily. "We shall be very happy here. I dread to think who he keeps 'His' and His' for, don't you?"

"I don't suppose the maid understands English," he said, but warming only slightly. "You don't expect to have to read off pillow-cases."

"I'm sure there *isn't* a maid."

"The bed is very small," he said.

"It'll be better than the car."

He thought, she is such a woman as I have never met. She's like a marvellous Tommy in the trenches—keeping everyone's pecker up. He hated Charlie for his luck.

I shan't ever be able to tell anybody about 'Hers' and 'Hers', Phyl thought regretfully—for she dearly loved to amuse their regulars back home. Given other circumstances, she might have worked up quite a story about it.

A tap on the door, and in came Mr Radam with two cups of tea on a tray. "I know you English," he said, rolling his eyes roguishly. "You can't be happy without your tea."

As neither of them ever drank it, they emptied the cups down the hand basin when he had gone.

Phyl opened the window and the sour, damp smell of new cement came up to her. All round about, building was going on; there was also the whine of a saw-mill, and a lot of clanking from the garage opposite. She leaned farther out, and then came back smiling into the room, and shut the window on the dust and noise. "He was quite right— that barman. You *can* see the sea from here. It's down the bottom of the street. Let's go and have a look as soon as we've unpacked."

On their way out of the hotel, they came upon Mr Radam, who was sitting in a broken old wicker chair, fanning himself with a folded newspaper.

"I shall prepare your dinner myself," he called after them. "And shall go now to make soup. I am a specialist of soup."

They strolled in the last of the sun by the glittering sea, looked at the painted boats, watched a man beating an octopus on a rock. Stanley bought her some lace-edged handkerchiefs, and even gave the lace-maker an extra five shillings, so that Phyl could pick a lemon off one of the trees in her garden. Each bought for the other a picture-postcard of the place, to keep.

"Well, it's been just about the best holiday I ever had," he said. "And there I was in half a mind not to come at all." He had for many years dreaded the holiday season, and only went away because everyone he knew did so.

"I just can't remember when I last had one," she said. There was not—never would be, he knew—the sound of self-pity in her voice.

This was only a small fishing-village; but on one of the headlands enclosing it and the harbour was a big new hotel, with balconies overlooking the sea, Phyl noted. They picked their way across a rubbly car-park and went in. Here, too, was the damp smell of cement; but there was a brightly-lighted empty bar with a small dance floor, and music playing.

"We could easily have got in here," Stanley said. "I'd like to wring that bloody barman's neck."

"He's probably some relation, trying to do his best."

"I'll best him."

They seemed to have spent a great deal of their time together hoisting themselves up on bar stools.

"Make them nice ones," Stanley added, ordering their drinks. Perhaps he feels a bit shy and awkward, too, Phyl thought.

"Not very busy," he remarked to the barman.

"In one week we close."

"Looks as if you've hardly opened," Stanley said, glancing round.

It's not *his* business to get huffy, Phyl thought indignantly, when the young man, not replying, shrugged and turned aside to polish some glasses. Customer's always right. He should know that. Politics, religion, colour-bar —however they argue together, they're all of them always right, and if you know your job you can joke them out of it and on to something safer. The times she had done that, making a fool of herself, no doubt, anything for peace and quiet. By the time the elections were over, she was usually worn out.

Stanley had hated her buying him a drink back in the hotel; but she had insisted. "What all that crowd would think of me!" she had said; but here, although it went much against her nature, she put aside her principles, and let him pay; let him set the pace, too. They became elated, and she was sure it would be all right—even having to go back to the soup-specialist's dinner. They might have avoided that; but too late now.

The barman, perhaps with a contemptuous underlining of their age, shuffled through some records and now put on *Night and Day*. For them both, it filled the bar with nostalgia.

"Come *on*!" said Stanley. "I've never danced with you. This always makes me feel . . . I don't know."

"Oh, I'm a terrible dancer," she protested. The Licensed Victuallers' Association annual dance was the only one she ever went to, and even there stayed in the bar most of the time. Laughing, however, she let herself be helped down off her stool.

He had once fancied himself a good dancer; but, in later years, got no practice, with Ethel being ill, and then dead. Phyl was surprised how light he was on his feet; he bounced her round, holding her firmly against his stomach, his hand pressed to her back, but gently, because of the sunburn. He had perfect rhythm and expertise, side-stepping, reversing, taking masterly control of her.

"Well, I never!" she cried. "You're making me quite breathless."

He rested his cheek against her hair, and closed his eyes, in the old, old way, and seemed to waft her away into a different dimension. It was then that he felt the first twinge, in his left toe. It was doom to him. He kept up the pace, but fell silent. When the record ended, he hoped that she would not want to stay on longer. To return to the hotel and take his gout pills was all he could think about. Some intuition made her refuse another drink. "We've got to go back to the soup-specialist some time," she said. "He might even be a good cook."

"Surprise, surprise!" Stanley managed to say, walking with pain towards the door.

Mr Radam was the most abominable cook. They had— in a large cold room with many tables—thin greasy chicken soup, and after that the chicken that had gone through the soup. Then peaches; he brought the tin and opened it before them, as if it were a precious wine, and no hanky-panky going on. He then stood over them, because he had much to say. "I was offered a post in Basingstoke. Two thousand pounds a year, and a car and a house thrown in. But what use is that to a man like me? Besides, Basingstoke has a most detestable climate."

Stanley sat, tight-lipped, trying not to lose his temper; but this man, and the pain, were driving him mad. He did not—dared not—drink any of the wine he had ordered.

"Yes, the Basingstoke employment I regarded as not *on*," Mr Radam said slangily.

Phyl secretly put out a foot and touched one of Stan's— the wrong one—and then thought he was about to have a heart attack. He screwed up his eyes and tried to breathe steadily, a slice of peach slithering about in his spoon. It was then she realised what was wrong with him.

"Oh, sod the peaches," she said cheerfully, when Mr Radam had gone off to make coffee, which would be the best they had ever tasted, he had promised. Phyl knew they would not complain about the horrible coffee that was coming. The more monstrous the egoist, she had observed from long practice, the more normal people hope to up-hold the fabrication—either for ease, or from a terror of any kind of collapse. She did not know. She was sure, though, as she praised the stringy chicken, hoisting the unlovable man's self-infatuation a notch higher, that she did so, because she feared him falling to pieces. Perhaps it was only fair, she decided, that weakness should get preferential treatment. Whether it would continue to do so, with Stanley's present change of mood, she was uncertain.

She tried to explain her thoughts to him when, he leaving his coffee, she having gulped hers down, they went to their bedroom. He nodded. He sat on the side of the bed, and put his face into his hands.

"Don't let's go out again," she said. "We can have a drink in here. I love a bedroom gin, and I brought a bottle in my case." She went busily to the wash-basin, and held up a dusty tooth-glass to the light.

"You have one," he said.

He was determined to keep unruffled, but every step she took across the uneven floorboards broke momentarily the steady pain into burning splinters.

"I've got gout," he said sullenly. "Bloody hell, I've got my gout."

"I thought so," she said. She put down the glass very quietly and came to him. "Where?"

He pointed down.

"Can you manage to get into bed by yourself?"

He nodded.

"Well, then!" she smiled. "Once you're in, I know what to do."

He looked up apprehensively, but she went almost on tiptoe out of the door and closed it softly.

He undressed, put on his pyjamas, and hauled himself onto the bed. When she came back, she was carrying two pillows. "Don't laugh, but they're 'His' and 'His'," she said. "Now, this is what I do for Charlie. I make a little pillow house for his foot, and it keeps the bedclothes off. Don't worry, I won't touch."

"On this one night," he said.

"You want to drink a lot of water." She put a glass beside him. " 'My husband's got a touch of gout,' I told them down there. And I really felt quite married to you when I said it."

She turned her back to him as she undressed. Her body,

set free at last, was creased with red marks, and across her shoulders the bright new skin from peeling had ragged, dirty edges of the old. She stretched her spine, put on a transparent night-gown and began to scratch her arms.

"Come here," he said, unmoving. "I'll do that."

So gently she pulled back the sheet and lay down beside him that he felt they had been happily married for years. The pang was that this was their only married night and his foot burned so that he thought that it would burst. And it will be a damn sight worse in the morning, he thought, knowing the pattern of his affliction. He began with one hand to stroke her itching arm.

Almost as soon as she had put the light off, an ominous sound zig-zagged about the room. Switching on again, she said, "I'll get that devil, if it's the last thing I do. You lie still."

She got out of bed again and ran round the room, slapping at the walls with her *Reader's Digest*, until at last she caught the mosquito, and Stanley's (as was apparent in the morning) blood squirted out.

After that, once more in the dark, they lay quietly. He endured his pain, and she without disturbing him rubbed her flaking skin.

"So this is our wicked adventure," he said bitterly to the moonlit ceiling.

"Would you rather be on your own?"

"No, no!" He groped with his hand towards her.

"Well, then . . ."

"How can you forgive me?"

"Let's worry about you, eh? Not me. That sort of thing

doesn't matter much to me nowadays. I only really do it to be matey. I don't know . . . by the time Charlie and I have locked up, washed up, done the till, had a bit of something to eat . . ."

Once, she had been as insatiable as a flame. She lay and remembered the days of her youth; but with interest, not wistfully.

Only once did she wake. It was the best night's sleep she'd had for a week. Moonlight now fell over the bed, and on one chalky white-washed wall. The sheet draped over them rose in a peak above his feet, so that he looked like a figure on a tomb. If Charlie could see me now, she suddenly thought. She tried not to have a fit of giggles for fear of shaking the bed. Stanley shifted, groaned in his sleep, then went on snoring, just as Charlie did.

He woke often during that night. The sheets were as abrasive as sandpaper. I knew this damn bed was too small, he thought. He shifted warily onto his side to look at Phyl who, in her sleep, made funny little whimpering sounds like a puppy. One arm flung above her head looked, in the moonlight, quite black against the pillow. Like going to bed with a coloured woman, he thought. He dutifully took a sip or two of water and then settled back again to endure his wakefulness.

"Well, *I* was happy," she said, wearing her emerald

124

green coat again, sitting next to him in the plane, fastening her safety-belt.

His face looked worn and grey.

"Don't mind me asking," she went on, "but did he charge for that tea we didn't order."

"Five shillings."

"I *knew* it. I wish you'd let me pay my share of everything. After all, it was me as well wanted to go."

He shook his head, smiling at her. In spite of his prediction, he felt better this departure afternoon, though tired and wary about himself.

"If only we were taking off on holiday now," he said. "not coming back. Why can't we meet up in Torquay or somewhere? Something for me to look forward to," he begged her, dabbing his mosquito-bitten forehead with his handkerchief.

"It was only my hysterectomy got me away this time," she said.

They ate, they drank, they held hands under a newspaper, and presently crossed the twilit coast of England, where farther along grey Hove was waiting for him. The trees had not changed colour much and only some—she noticed, as she looked down on them, coming in to land— were yellower.

She knew that it was worse for him. He had to return to his empty flat; she, to a full bar, and on a Saturday, too. She wished there was something she could do to send him off cheerful.

"To me," she said, having refastened her safety-belt, taking his hand again. "To me, it was lovely. To me it was just as good as if we had."

Sisters

ON a Thursday morning, soon after Mrs Mason returned from shopping—in fact she had not yet taken off her hat—a neat young man wearing a dark suit and spectacles, half-gold, half-mock tortoiseshell, and carrying a rolled umbrella, called at the house, and brought her to the edge of ruin. He gave a name, which meant nothing to her, and she invited him in, thinking he was about insurance, or someone from her solicitor. He stood in the sitting-room, looking keenly about him, until she asked him to sit down and tell her his business.

"Your sister," he began. "Your sister Marion," and Mrs Mason's hand flew up to her cheek. She gazed at him in alarmed astonishment, then closed her eyes.

In this town, where she had lived all her married life, Mrs Mason was respected, even mildly loved. No one had a word to say against her, so it followed there were no strong feelings either way. She seemed to have been made for widowhood, and had her own little set, for bridge and coffee mornings, and her committee-meetings for the better known charities—such as the National Society for the Prevention of Cruelty to Children, and the Royal Society for the Prevention of Cruelty to Animals.

Her husband had been a successful dentist, and when he died she moved from the house where he had had his practice, into a smaller one in a quiet road nearby. She had no money worries, no worries of any kind. Childless and serene, she lived from day to day. They were almost able to set their clocks by her, her neighbours said, seeing her leaving the house in the mornings, for shopping and coffee at the Oak Beams Tea Room, pushing a basket on wheels, stalking rather on high-heeled shoes, blue-rinsed, rouged. Her front went down in a straight line from her heavy bust, giving her a stately look, the weight throwing her back a little. She took all of life at the same pace—a sign of ageing. She had settled to it a long time ago, and all of her years seemed the same now, although days had slightly varying patterns. Hers was mostly a day-time life, for it was chiefly a woman's world she had her place in. After tea, her friends' husbands came home, and then Mrs Mason pottered in her garden, played patience in the winter, or read historical romances from the library. "Something light," she would tell the assistant, as if seeking suggestions from a waiter. She could never remember the names of authors or their works, and it was quite a little disappointment when she discovered that she had read a novel before. She had few other disappointments—nothing much more than an unexpected shower of rain, or a tough cutlet, or the girl at the hairdresser's getting her rinse wrong.

Mrs Mason had always done, and still did, everything expected of women in her position—which was a phrase she often used. She baked beautiful Victoria sponges for bring-and-buy sales, arranged flowers, made *gros-point* covers for her chairs, gave tea-parties, even sometimes, daringly, sherry-parties with one or two husbands there, much against their will—but this was kept from her. She was occasionally included in other woman's evening gatherings for she made no difference when there was a crowd, and it was an easy kindness. She mingled, and chatted about other people's holidays and families and jobs. She never drank more than two glasses of sherry, and was a good guest, always exclaiming appreciatively at the sight of canapes, "My goodness, *someone's* been busy!"

Easefully the time had gone by.

This Thursday morning, the young man, having mentioned her sister, and seen her distress, glanced at one of the needlework cushions, and rose for a moment to examine it. Having ascertained that it was her work (a brief, distracted nod), he praised it, and sat down again. Then, thinking the pause long enough, he said, "I am writing a book about your sister, and I did so hope for some help from you."

"How did you know?" she managed to ask with her numbed lips. "That she was, I mean."

He smiled modestly. "It was a matter of literary detection—my great hobby. My life's work, I might say."

He had small, even teeth, she noticed, glancing at him quickly. They glinted, like his spectacles, the buttons on his jacket and the signet ring on his hand. He was a hideously glinty young man she decided, looking away again.

"I have nothing to say of any interest."

"But anything you say will interest us."

"Us?"

"Her admirers. The reading public. Well, the world at large." He shrugged.

"The world at large" was menacing, for it included this

town where Mrs Mason lived. It included the Oak Beams
Tea Room, and the Societies of Prevention.

"I have nothing to say." She moved, as if she would
rise.

"Come! You had your childhoods together. We know
about those only from the stories. The beautiful stories.
That wonderful house by the sea."

He looked at a few shelves of books beside him, and
seemed disappointed. They were her late husband's books
about military history.

"It wasn't so wonderful," she said, for she disliked all
exaggeration. "It was a quite ordinary, shabby house."

"Yes?" he said softly, settling back in his chair and
clasping his ladylike hands.

The shabby, ordinary house—the Rectory—had a path
between cornfields to the sea. On either side of it now were
caravan sites. Her husband, Gerald, had taken her back
there once when they were on holiday in Cornwall. He,
of course, had been in the know. She had been upset about
the caravans, and he had comforted her. She wished that he
were here this morning to deal with this terrifying young
man.

Of her childhood, she remembered—as one does—
mostly the still hot afternoons, the cornflowers and thistles
and scarlet pimpernels, the scratchy grass against her bare
legs as they went down to the beach. Less clearly, she re-
called evenings with shadows growing longer, and far-off
sounding voices calling across the garden. She could see
the picture of the house with windows open, and towels

and bathing-costumes drying on upstairs sills and canvas shoes, newly-whitened, drying too, in readiness for the next day's tennis. It had all been so familiar and comforting; but her sister, Marion, had complained of dullness, had ungratefully chafed and rowed and rebelled—although using it all (twisting it) in later years to make a name for herself. It had never, never been as she had written of it. And she, Mrs Mason, the little Cassie of those books, had never been at all that kind of child. These, more than forty years after, she still shied away from that description of her squatting and peeing into a rock-pool, in front of some little boys Marion had made up. "Cassie! Cassie!" her sisters had cried, apparently, in consternation. But it was Marion herself who had done that, more like. There were a few stories she could have told about Marion, if she had been the one to expose them all to shame, she thought grimly. The rock-pool episode was nothing, really, compared with some of the other inventions—'experiments with sex', as reviewers had described them at the time. It was as if her sister had been compelled to set her sick fancies against a background that she knew.

Watching Mrs Mason's face slowly flushing all over to blend with her rouged cheekbones, the young man, leaning back easily, felt he had bided his time long enough. Something was obviously being stirred up. He said gently —so that his words seemed to come to her like her own thoughts—"A few stories now, please. Was it a happy childhood?"

"Yes. No. It was just an ordinary childhood."

"With such a genius amongst you? How *awfully* interesting!"

"She was no different from any of the rest of us." But she *had* been, and so unpleasantly, as it turned out.

"Really *extraordinarily* interesting." He allowed himself to lean forward a little, then, wondering if the slightest show of eagerness might silence her, he glanced about the room again. There were only two photographs—one of a long-ago bride and bridegroom, the other of a pompous-looking man with some sort of chain of office hanging on his breast.

It was proving very hard-going, this visit; but all the more of a challenge for that.

Mrs Mason, in her silvery-grey wool dress, suddenly seemed to him to resemble an enormous salmon. She even had a salmon shape—thick from the shoulders down and tapering away to surprisingly tiny, out-turned feet. He imagined trying to land her. She was demanding all the skill and tenacity he had. This was very pleasurable. Having let him in, and sat down, her good manners could find no way of getting rid of him. He was sure of that. Her good manners were the only encouraging thing, so far.

"You know, you are really not at all what I expected," he said boldly, admiringly. "Not in the very least like your sister, are you?"

What he had expected was an older version of the famous photograph in the Collected Edition—that waif-like creature with the fly-away fringe and great dark eyes.

Mrs Mason now carefully lifted off her hat, as if it were a coronet. Then she touched her hair, pushing it up a little. "I was the pretty one," she did not say; but, feeling some explanation was asked for, told him what all the world knew. "My sister had poor health," she said. "Asthma and migraines, and so on. Lots of what we now call allergies. I never had more than a couple of days' illness in my life." She remembered Marion always being fussed over—wheezing and puking and whining, or stamping her feet up and down in temper and frustration, causing scenes, a general rumpus at any given moment.

He longed to get inside her mind; for interesting things were going on there he guessed. Patience, he thought, regarding her. She was wearing opaque grey stockings; to hide varicose veins, he thought. He knew everything about women, and mentally unclothed her. In a leisurely fashion—since he would not hurry anything—he stripped off her peach-coloured slip and matching knickers, tugged her out of her sturdy corselette, whose straps had bitten deep into her plump shoulders, leaving a permanent indentation. He did not even jib at the massive, mottled flesh beneath, creased, as it must be, from its rigid confinement, or the suspender imprints at the top of her tapering legs. Her navel would be full of talcum powder.

"It was all so long ago. I don't want to be reminded," she said simply.

"Have you any photographs—holiday snapshots, for instance? I adore looking at old photographs."

There was a boxful upstairs, faded sepia scenes of them all paddling—dresses tucked into bloomers—or picnicking, with sandwiches in hand, and feet out of focus. Her father, the Rector, had developed and printed the photographs himself, and they had not lasted well. "I don't care to live in the past," was all she said in reply.

"Were you and Marion close to one another?"

"We were sisters," she said primly.

"And you kept in touch? I should think that you enjoyed basking in the reflected glory." He knew that she had not kept in touch, and was sure by now that she had done no basking.

"She went to live in Paris, as no doubt you know."

Thank heavens, Mrs Mason had always thought, that she *had* gone to live in Paris, and that she herself had married and been able to change her name. Still quite young, and before the war, Marion had died. It was during Mr Mason's year as mayor. They had told no one.

"Did you ever meet Godwin? Or any of that set?"

"Of course not. My husband wouldn't have had them in the house."

The young man nodded.

Oh, that dreadful clique. She was ashamed to have it mentioned to her by someone of the opposite sex, a complete stranger. She had been embarrassed to speak of it to her own husband, who had been so extraordinarily kind and forgiving about everything connected with Marion. But that raffish life in Paris in the thirties! Her sister living with the man Godwin or, turn and turn about with others of her set. They all had switched from one partner to the other; sometimes—she clasped her hands together so tightly that her rings hurt her fingers—to others of the same sex. She knew about it; the world knew; no doubt her friends knew, although it was not the sort of thing they would have discussed. Books had been written about that Paris lot, as Mrs Mason thought of them, and their correspondence published. Godwin, and Miranda Braun, the

painter, and Grant Opie, the American, who wrote ob-
scene books; and many of the others. They were all
notorious: that was Mrs Mason's word for them.

"I think she killed my father," she said in a low voice,
almost as if she were talking to herself. "He fell ill, and did
not seem to want to go on living. He would never have her
name mentioned, or any of her books in the house. She
sent him a copy of the first one—she had left home by then,
and was living in London. He read some of it, then took it
out to the incinerator in the garden and burned it. I remember it now, his face was as white as a sheet."

"But *you* have read the books surely?" he asked, playing
her in gently.

She nodded, looking ashamed. "Yes, later, I did." A
terrified curiosity had proved too strong to resist. And,
reading, she had discovered a childhood she could hardly
recognise, although it was all there: all the pieces were
there, but shifted round as in a kaleidoscope. Worse came
after the first book, the stories of their girlhood and growing up and falling in love. She, the Cassie of the books, had
become a well-known character, with all her secrets laid
bare; though they were really the secrets of Marion herself
and not those of the youngest sister. The candour had
caused a stir in those far-off days. During all the years of
public interest, Mrs Mason had kept her silence, and
lately had been able to bask indeed—in the neglect which
had fallen upon her sister, as it falls upon most great writers
at some period after their death. It was done with and laid
to rest, she had thought—until this morning.

"And you didn't think much of them, I infer," the
young man said.

She started, and looked confused. "Of what?" she asked, drawing back, tightening his line.

"Your sister's stories."

"They weren't true. We were well-brought-up girls."

"Your other sister died, too."

He *had* been rooting about, she thought in dismay. "She died before all the scandal," Mrs Mason said grimly. "She was spared."

The telephone rang in the hall, and she murmured politely and got up. He heard her, in a different, chatty voice, making arrangements and kind enquiries, actually laughing. She rang off presently, and then stood for a moment steadying herself. She peered into a glass and touched her hair again. Full of strength and resolution, she went back to the sitting-room and just caught him clipping a pen back into the inside of his jacket.

"I'm afraid I shall have to get on with some jobs now," she said clearly, and remained standing.

He rose—had to—cursing the telephone for ringing, just when he was bringing her in so beautifully. "And you are sure you haven't even one little photograph to lend me," he asked. "I would take enormous care of it."

"Yes, I am quite sure." She was like another woman now. She had been in touch with her own world, and had gained strength from it.

"Then may I come to see you again when you are not so busy?"

"Oh, no, I don't think so." She put out an arm and held the door-handle. "I really don't think there would be any point."

He really felt himself that there would not be. Still

looking greedily about him, he went into the hall towards
the front door. He had the idea of leaving his umbrella
behind, so that he would have to return for it; but she
firmly handed it to him. Even going down the path to the
gate, he seemed to be glancing from side to side, as if
memorising the names of flowers.

"I said nothing, I said nothing," Mrs Mason kept telling
herself, on her way that afternoon to play bridge. "I
merely conveyed my disapproval." But she had a flustered
feeling that her husband would not have agreed that she
had done only that. And she guessed that the young man
would easily make something of nothing. "She killed my
father." She had said that. It would be in print, with her
name attached to it. He had been clever to ferret her out,
the menacing young man and now he had something new
to offer to the world—herself. What else had she said, for
heaven's sake? She was walking uphill, and panted a little.
She could not for the life of her remember if she had said
any more. But, ah yes! How her father had put that book
into the incinerator. Just like Hitler, some people would
think. And her name and Marion's would be linked together. Ex-mayoress, and that rackety and lustful set.
Some of her friends would be openly cool, others too kind,
all of them shocked. They would discuss the matter behind her back. There were even those who would say they
were 'intrigued' and ask questions.

Mrs Oldfellow, Mrs Fitch and Miss Christy all thought
she played badly that afternoon, especially Mrs Oldfellow
who was her partner. She did not stay for sherry when the

bridge was over but excused herself, saying that she felt a cold coming on. Mrs Fitch's offer to run her back in the car she refused, hoping that the fresh air might clear her head.

She walked home in her usual sedate way; but she could not rid herself of the horrible idea they were talking about her already.

Hôtel du Commerce

THE hallway, with its reception desk and hat-stand, was gloomy. Madame Bertail reached up to the board where the keys hung, took the one for Room Eight, and led the way upstairs. Her daughter picked up the heavier suitcase, and begun to lurch lopsidedly across the hall with it until Leonard, blushing as he always (and under-standably) did when he was obliged to speak French, in-sisted on taking it from her.

Looking offended, she grabbed instead Melanie's spank-ing-new wedding-present suitcase, and followed them grimly, as *they* followed Madame Bertail's stiffly corseted back. Level with her shoulder-blades, the corsets stopped and the massive flesh moved gently with each step she took, as if it had a life of its own.

In Room Eight was a small double bed and wallpaper with a paisley pattern, on which what looked like curled-up blood-red embryos were repeated every two inches upon a sage-green background. There were other patterns for curtains and chair covers and the thin eiderdown. It was a depressing room, and a smell of some previous occupier's *Ambre Solaire* still hung about it.

"I'm so sorry, darling," Leonard apologised, as soon as they were alone.

Melanie smiled. For a time, they managed to keep up their spirits. "I'm so tired, I'll sleep anywhere," she said, not knowing about the mosquito hidden in the curtains, or the lumpiness of the bed, and other horrors to follow.

They were both tired. A day of driving in an open car had made them feel, now they had stopped, quite dull and drowsy. Conversation was an effort.

Melanie opened her case. There was still confetti about. A crescent-shaped white piece fluttered onto the carpet, and she bent quickly and picked it up. So much about honeymoons was absurd—even little reminders like this one. And there had been awkwardnesses they could never have foreseen—especially that of having to make their way in a foreign language. (*Lune de miel* seemed utterly improbable to her.) She did not know how to ask a maid to wash a blouse, although she had pages of irregular verbs somewhere in her head, and odd words, from lists she had learned as a child—the Parts of the Body, the Trees of the Forest, the Days of the Week—would often spring gratifyingly to her rescue.

When she had unpacked, she went to the window and leaned out, over a narrow street with lumpy cobbles all ready for an early-morning din of rattling carts and slipping hooves.

Leonard kept glancing nervously at her as he unpacked. He did everything methodically, and at one slow pace. She was quick and untidy, and spent much time hanging about waiting for him, growing depressed, then exasperated, leaning out of windows, as now, strolling impatiently in gardens.

He smoked in the bedroom: she did not, and often thought it would have been better the other way about, so that she could have had something to do while she waited.

He hung up his dressing-gown, paused, then trod

heavily across to his suitcase and took out washing things, which he arranged neatly on a shelf. He looked at her again. Seen from the back, hunched over the window-sill, she seemed to be visibly drooping, diminishing, like melting wax; and he knew that her mood was because of him. But a lifetime's habit—more than that, something inborn—made him feel helpless. He also had a moment of irritation himself, seeing her slippers thrown anyhow under a chair.

"Ready, then," he said, in a tone of anticipation and decision.

She turned eagerly from the window, and saw him take up his comb. He stood before the glass, combing, combing his thin hair, lapsing once more into dreaminess, intent on what he was doing. She sighed quietly and turned back to look out of the window.

"I can see a spire of the Cathedral," she said presently; but her head was so far out of the window—and a lorry was going by—that he did not hear her.

Well, we've *had* the Cathedral, she thought crossly. It was too late for the stained glass. She would never be able to make him see that every minute counted, or that there should not be some preordained method but, instead, a shifting order of priorities. Unpacking can wait; but the light will not.

By the time they got out for their walk, and saw the Cathedral, it was floodlit, bone-white against the dark sky, bleached, flat, stagey, though beautiful in this unintended and rather unsuitable way. Walking in the twisting streets, Leonard and Melanie had glimpsed the one tall spire above roof-tops, then lost it. Arm-in-arm, they had stopped to look in shop windows, at glazed pigs trotters, tarts full of neatly arranged strawberries, sugared almonds on stems, in bunches, tied with ribbons. Leonard lingered, comparing prices of watches and cameras with those at home in England; Melanie, feeling chilly, tried gently to draw him on. At last, without warning, they came to the square where the Cathedral stood, and here there were more shops, all full of little plaster statues and rosaries, and antiques for the tourists.

"Exorbitant," Leonard kept saying. "My God, how they're out to fleece you!"

Melanie stood staring up at the Cathedral until her neck ached. The great rose window was dark, the light glaring on the stone façade too static. The first sense of amazement and wonder faded. It was part of her impatient nature to care most for first impressions. On their way south, the sudden, and far-away sight of Chartres Cathedral across the plain, crouched on the horizon, with its lop-sided spires, like a giant hare, had meant much more to her than the close-up details of it. Again, for *that*, they had been too late. Before they reached the town, storm-clouds had gathered. It might as well have been dusk inside the Cathedral. She, for her part, would not have stopped to fill up with petrol on the road. She would have risked it, parked the car anywhere, and run.

Staring up at *this* Cathedral, she felt dizzy from leaning backwards, and swayed suddenly, and laughed. He caught her close to him and so, walking rather unevenly, with arms about the other's waist, moved on, out of the square, and back to the hotel.

Such moments, of more-than-usual love, gave them

both great confidence. This time, their mood of elation lasted much longer than a moment.

Although the hotel dining-room was dark, and they were quite alone in it, speaking in subdued voices, their humour held; and held, as they took their key from impassive Madame Bertail, who still sat at the desk, doing her accounts; it even held as they undressed in their depressing room, and had no need to hold longer than that. Once in bed, they had always been safe.

"Don't tell me! Don't tell me!"

They woke at the same instant and stared at the darkness, shocked, wondering where they were.

"Don't tell me! I'll spend my money how I bloody well please."

The man's voice, high and hysterical, came through the wall, just behind their heads.

A woman was heard laughing softly, with obviously affected amusement.

Something was thrown, and broke.

"I've had enough of your nagging."

"I've had enough of *you*," the woman answered coolly.

Melanie buried her head against Leonard's shoulder and he put an arm round her.

"I had enough of *you*, a very long time ago," the woman's voice went on. "I can't honestly remember a time when I *hadn't* had enough of you."

"What I've gone through!"

"What *you've* gone through?"

"Yes, that's what I said. What *I've* gone through."

"Don't shout. It's so common." She had consciously lowered her own voice, then said, forgetting, in almost a shout, "It's a pity for both our sakes, you were so greedy. For Daddy's money, I mean. That's all you ever cared about—my father's money."

"All *you* cared about was getting into bed with me."

"You great braggart. I've always loathed going to bed with you. Who wouldn't?"

Leonard heaved himself up in bed, and knocked on the damp wallpaper.

"I always felt sick," the woman's voice went on, taking no notice. She was as strident now as the man; had begun to lose her grip on the situation, as he had done. "And God knows," she said, "how many other women you've made feel sick."

Leonard knocked louder, with his fist this time. The wall seemed as soft as if it were made from cardboard.

"I'm scared," said Melanie. She sat up and switched on the light. "Surely he'll kill her, if she goes on like that."

"You little strumpet!" The man slurred this word, tried to repeat it and dried up, helplessly, goaded into incoherence.

"Be careful! Just be careful!" A dangerous, deliberate voice hers was now.

"Archie Durrant? Do you think I didn't know about Archie Durrant? Don't take me for a fool."

"I'll warn you; don't put ideas into my head, my precious husband. At least Archie Durrant wouldn't bring me to a lousy place like this."

She then began to cry. They reversed their rôles and he in his turn became the cool one.

"He won't take you anywhere, my pet. Like me, he's had enough. *Un*like me, *he* can skedaddle."

"Why doesn't someone *do* something!" asked Melanie, meaning, of course, that Leonard should. "Everyone must be able to hear. And they're English, too. It's so shaming, and horrible."

"Go on, then, skedaddle, skedaddle!" The absurd word went on and on, blurred, broken by sobs. Something more was thrown—something with a sharp, hard sound; perhaps a shoe or book.

Leonard sprang out of bed and put on his dressing-gown and slippers.

Slippers! thought Melanie, sitting up in bed, shivering.

As Leonard stepped out into the passage, he saw Madame Bertail coming along it, from the other direction. She, too, wore a dressing-gown, corded round her stout stomach: her grey hair was thinly braided. She looked steadily at Leonard, as if dismissing him, classing him with his loose compatriots, then knocked quickly on the door and at once tried the door-handle. The key had been turned in the lock. She knocked again, and there was silence inside the room. She knocked once more, very loudly, as if to make sure of this silence, and then, without a word to Leonard, seeming to feel satisfied that she had dealt successfully with the situation, she went off down the corridor.

Leonard went back to the bedroom and slowly took off his dressing-gown and slippers.

"I think that will be that," he said, and got back into bed and tried to warm poor Melanie.

"You talk about your father's money," the man's voice went on, almost at once. "But I wouldn't want any truck with that kind of money."

"You just want it."

Their tone was more controlled, as if they were temporarily calmed. However, although the wind had dropped they still quietly angled for it, keeping things going for the time being.

"I'll never forget the first time I realised how you got on my nerves," he said, in the equable voice of an old friend reminiscing about happier days. "That way you walk upstairs with your bottom waggling from side to side. My God, I've got to walk upstairs and downstairs behind that bottom for the rest of my life, I used to think."

Such triviality! Melanie thought fearfully, pressing her hands against her face. To begin with such a thing—for the hate to grow from it—not nearly as bad as being slow and keeping people waiting.

"I wasn't seriously loathing you then," the man said in a conversational tone. "Even after that fuss about Archie Durrant. I didn't seriously *hate* you."

"Thank you very much, you . . . cuckold."

If Leonard did not snore at that moment, he certainly breathed sonorously.

During that comparative lull in the next room, he had dropped off to sleep, leaving Melanie wakeful and afraid.

"She called him a cuckold," she hissed into Leonard's ear.

"No, the time, I think," said the man behind the wall, in the same deadly flat voice, "the time I first really hated you, was when you threw the potatoes at me."

"Oh, yes, that was a *great* evening," she said, in tones chiming with affected pleasure.

"In front of my own mother."

"She seemed to enjoy it as much as I did. Probably longed for years to do it herself."

"That was when I first realised."

"Why did you stay?" There was silence. Then, "Why stay now? Go on! Go now! I'll help you to pack. There's your bloody hairbrush for a start. My God, you look ridiculous when you duck down like that. You sickening little coward."

"I'll kill you."

"Oh God, he'll kill her," said Melanie, shaking Leonard roughly.

"You won't, you know," shouted the other woman.

The telephone rang in the next room.

"Hallo?" The man's voice was cautious, ruffled. The receiver was quietly replaced. "You see what you've done?" he said. "Someone ringing up to complain about the noise you're making."

"You don't think I give a damn for anyone in a crumby little hotel like this, do you?"

"Oh, my nerves, my nerves, my nerves," the man suddenly groaned. Bed-springs creaked, and Melanie imagined him sinking down on the edge of the bed, his face buried in his hands.

Silence lasted only a minute or two. Leonard was fast asleep now. Melanie lay very still, listening to a mosquito coming and going above her head.

Then the crying began, at first a little sniffing, then a quiet sobbing.

"Leonard, you must wake up. I can't lie here alone listening to it. Or *do* something, for heaven's sake."

He put out a hand, as if to stave her off, or calm her, without really disturbing his sleep, and this gesture infuriated her. She slapped his hand away roughly.

"There's nothing I can do," he said, still clinging to the idea of sleep; then, as she flounced over in the bed, turning her back to him, he resignedly sat up and turned on the light. Blinking and tousled, he stared before him, and then leaned over and knocked on the wall once more.

"*That* won't do any good," said Melanie.

"Well, their door's locked, so what else can I do?"

"Ring up the police."

"I can't do that. Anyhow, I don't know how to in French."

"Well, try. If the hotel was on fire, you'd do something, wouldn't you?"

Her sharp tone was new to him, and alarming.

"It's not really our business."

"If he kills her? While you were asleep, she called him a cuckold. I thought he was going to kill her then. And even if he doesn't, we can't hope to get any sleep. It's perfectly horrible. It sounds like a child crying."

"Yes, with temper. Your feet are frozen."

"Of course, they're frozen." Her voice blamed him for this.

"My dear, don't let *us* quarrel."

"I'm so tired. Oh, that—damned mosquito." She sat up, and tried to smack it against the wall, but it had gone. "It's been such an awful day."

"I thought it was a perfectly beautiful day."

She pressed her lips together and closed her eyes, drawing herself away from him, as if determined now, somehow or other, to go to sleep.

"Didn't you like your day?" he asked.

"Well, you must have known I was disappointed about the Cathedral. Getting there when it was too dark."

"I didn't know. You didn't give me an inkling. We can go first thing in the morning."

"It wouldn't be the same. Oh, you're so hopeless. You hang about, and hang about, and drive me mad with impatience."

She lay on her side, well away from him on the very edge of the bed, facing the horribly patterned curtains, her mouth so stiff, her eyes full of tears. He made an attempt to draw her close, but she became rigid, her limbs were iron.

"You see, she's quietening down," he said. The weeping had gone through every stage—from piteous sobbing, gasping, angry moans, to—now—a lulled whimpering, dying off, hardly heard. And the man was silent. Had he dropped senseless across the bed, Melanie wondered, or was he still sitting there, staring at the picture of his own despair.

"I'm so sorry about the Cathedral. I had no idea . . ." said Leonard, switching off the light, and sliding down in bed. Melanie kept her cold feet to herself.

"We'll say no more about it," she said, in a grim little voice.

They slept late. When he awoke, Leonard saw that Melanie was almost falling out of bed in her attempt to keep away from him. Disquieting memories made him frown. He tried to lay his thoughts out in order. The voices in the next room, the nightmare of weeping and abuse; but worse, Melanie's cold voice, her revelation of that harboured disappointment; then, worse again, even worse, her impatience with him. He drove her nearly mad, she had said. Always? Since they were married? When?

At last Melanie awoke, and seemed uncertain of how to behave. Unable to make up her mind, she assumed a sort of non-behaviour to be going on with, which he found most mystifying.

"Shall we go to the Cathedral?" he asked.

"Oh, I don't think so," she said carelessly. She even turned her back to him while she dressed.

There was silence from the next room, but neither of them referred to it. It was as if some shame of their own were shut up in there. The rest of the hotel was full of noises—kitchen clatterings and sharp voices. A vacuum cleaner bumped and whined along the passage outside, and countrified traffic went by in the cobbled street.

Melanie's cheeks and forehead were swollen with mosquito bites, which gave her an angry look. She scratched one on her wrist and made it water. They seemed the stigmata of her irritation.

They packed their cases.

"Ready?" he asked.

"When you are," she said sullenly.

"Might as well hit the trail as soon as we've had breakfast," he said, trying to sound optimistic, as if nothing were wrong. He had no idea of how they would get through the day. They had no plans, and she seemed disinclined to discuss any.

They breakfasted in silence in the empty dining-room. Some of the tables had chairs stacked on them.

"You've no idea where you want to go, then?" he asked.

She was spreading apricot jam on a piece of bread and he leaned over and gently touched her hand. She laid down the knife, and put her hand in her lap. Then picked up the bread with her left hand and began to eat.

They went upstairs, to fetch their cases and, going along the passage, could see that the door of the room next to theirs now stood wide open. Before they reached it, a woman came out and hesitated in the doorway, looking back into the room. There was an appearance of brightness about her—her glowing face, shining hair, starched dress. Full of gay anticipation as it was, her voice, as she called back into the room, was familiar to Melanie and Leonard.

"Ready, darling?"

The other familiar voice replied. The man came to the doorway, carrying the case. He put his arm round the woman's waist and they went off down the passage. Such a well turned-out couple, Melanie thought, staring after them, as she paused at her own doorway, scratching her mosquito bites.

"Let's go to that marvellous place for lunch," she heard the man suggesting. They turned a corner to the landing, but as they went on downstairs, their laughter floated up after them.

Miss A. and Miss M.

A NEW motorway had made a different landscape of that part of England I loved as a child, cutting through meadows, spanning valleys, shaving off old gardens and leaving houses perched on islands of confusion. Nothing is recognisable now: the guesthouse has gone, with its croquet-lawn; the cherry orchard; and Miss Alliot's and Miss Martin's week-end cottage. I should think that little is left anywhere, except in *my* mind.

I was a town child, and the holidays in the country had a sharp delight which made the waiting time of school term, of traffic, of leaflessness, the unreal part of my life. At Easter, and for weeks in the summer, sometimes even for a few snatched days in winter, we drove out there to stay—it wasn't far—for my mother loved the country, too, and in that place we had put down roots.

St Margaret's was the name of the guest-house, which was run by two elderly ladies who had come down in the world, bringing with them quantities of heavily riveted Crown Derby, and silver plate. Miss Louie and Miss Beatrice.

My mother and I shared a bedroom with a sloping floor and threadbare carpet. The wallpaper had faint roses, and a powdery look from damp. Oil lamps or candles lit the rooms, and, even now, the smell of paraffin brings it back, that time of my life. We were in the nineteen twenties.

Miss Beatrice, with the help of a maid called Mabel,

cooked deliciously. Beautiful creamy porridge, I remember, and summer puddings, suckling pigs and maids-of-honour and marrow jam. The guests sat at one long table with Miss Louie one end and Miss Beatrice the other, and Mabel scuttling in and out with silver domed dishes. There was no wine. No one drank anything alcoholic, that I remember. Sherry was kept for trifle, and that was it, and the new world of cocktail parties was elsewhere.

The guests were for the most part mild, bookish people who liked a cheap and quiet holiday—schoolmasters, elderly spinsters, sometimes people to do with broadcasting who, in those days, were held in awe. The guests returned, so that we had constant friends among them, and looked forward to our reunions. Sometimes there were other children. If there were not, I did not care. I had Miss Alliot and Miss Martin.

These two were always spoken of in that order, and not because it was easier to say like that, or more euphonious. They appeared at luncheon and supper, but were not guests. At the far end of the orchard they had a cottage for weekends and holidays. They were schoolmistresses in London.

'Cottage' is not quite the word for what was little more than a wooden shack with two rooms and a verandah. It was called Breezy Lodge, and draughts did blow between its ramshackle clap-boarding.

Inside, it was gay, for Miss Alliot was much inclined to orange and yellow and grass-green, and the cane chairs had cushions patterned with nasturtiums and marigolds and ferns. The curtains and her clothes reflected the same taste.

Miss Martin liked misty blues and greys, though it barely mattered that she did. She had a small smudged-looking face with untidy eyebrows, a gentle, even submerged nature. She was a great—but quiet—reader and never seemed to wish to talk of what she had read. Miss Alliot, on the other hand, would occasionally skim through a book and find enough in it for long discourses and an endless supply of allusions. She wrung the most out of everything she did or saw and was a great talker.

That was a time when one fell in love with who ever was *there*. In my adolescence the only males available to me for adoration were such as Shelley or Rupert Brooke or Owen Nares. A rather more real passion could be lavished on prefects at school or the younger mistresses.

Miss Alliot was heaven-sent, it seemed to me. She was a holiday goddess. Miss Martin was just a friend. She tried to guide my reading, as an elder sister might. This was a new relationship to me. I had no elder sister, and I had sometimes thought that to have had one would have altered my life entirely, and whether for better or worse I had never been able to decide.

How I stood with Miss Alliot was a reason for more pondering. Why did she take trouble over me, as she did? I considered myself sharp for my age: now I see that I was sharp only for the age I *lived* in. Miss Alliot cultivated me to punish Miss Martin—as if she needed another weapon. I condoned the punishing. I basked in the doing of it. I turned my own eyes from the troubled ones under the fuzzy brows, and I pretended not to know precisely what was being done. Flattery nudged me on. Not physically fondled, I was fondled all the same.

In those days before—more than forty years before—
the motorway, that piece of countryside was beautiful, and
the word 'countryside' still means there to me. The Chil-
tern Hills. Down one of those slopes below St Margaret's
streamed the Cherry Orchard, a vast delight in summer of
marjoram and thyme. An unfrequented footpath led
through it, and every step was aromatic. We called this
walk the Echo Walk—down through the trees and up
from the valley on its other side to larch woods.

Perched on a stile at the edge of the wood, one called
out messages to be rung back across the flinty valley.
Once, alone, I called out, "I love you," loud and strong,
and "I love you" came back faint, and mocking. "Miss
Alliot," I added. But that response was blurred. Perhaps
I feared to shout too loudly, or it was not a good echo
name. I tried no others.

On Sunday mornings I walked across the fields to
church with Miss Martin. Miss Alliot would not join us.
It was scarcely an intellectual feast, she said, or spiritually
uplifting, with the poor old Vicar mumbling on and the
organ asthmatic. In London, she attended St Ethelburga's
in the Strand, and spoke a great deal of a Doctor Cobb.
But, still more, she spoke of the Townsends.

For she punished Miss Martin with the Townsends too.

The Townsends lived in Northumberland. Their country house was grand, as was to be seen in photographs.
Miss Alliot appeared in some of these shading her eyes as
she lay back in a deck-chair in a sepia world or—with
Suzanne Lenglen bandeau and accordion-pleated dress—
simply standing, to be photographed. By whom? I wondered. Miss Martin wondered, too, I thought.

Once a year, towards the end of the summer holiday (mine: theirs) Miss Alliot was invited to take the train North. We knew that she would have taken that train at an hour's notice, and, if necessary, have dropped everything for the Townsends.

What they consisted of—the Townsends—I was never really sure. It was a group name, both in my mind and in our conversations. "Do the Townsends play croquet?" I enquired, or "Do the Townsends change for dinner?" I was avid for information. It was readily given.

"I know what the Townsends would think of *her*," Miss Alliot said, of the only common woman, as she put it, who had ever stayed at St Margaret's. Mrs Price came with her daughter, Muriel, who was seven years old and had long, burnished plaits, which she would toss—one, then the other—over her shoulders. Under Miss Alliot's guidance, I scorned both Mrs Price and child, and many a laugh we had in Breezy Lodge at their expense. Scarcely able to speak for laughter, Miss Alliot would recount her 'gems', as she called them. "Oh, she *said* . . . one can't believe it, little Muriel . . . Mrs Price *insists* on it . . . changes her socks and knickers twice a day. She likes her to be nice and fresh. And . . ." Miss Alliot was a good mimic, " 'she always takes an apple for recess'. What in God's name is recess?"

This was rather strong language for those days, and I admired it.

"It's 'break' or . . ." Miss Martin began reasonably.

This was her mistake. She slowed things up with her reasonableness, when what Miss Alliot wanted, and I wanted, was a flight of fancy.

I tried, when those two were not there, to gather foolish or despicable phrases from Mrs Price, but I did not get far. (I suspect now Miss Alliot's inventive mind at work— rehearsing for the Townsends.)

All these years later, I have attempted, while writing this, to be fair to Mrs Price, almost forgotten for forty years; but even without Miss Alliot's direction I think I should have found her tiresome. She boasted to my mother (and no adult was safe from my eavesdropping) about her hysterectomy, and the gynaecologist who doted on her. "I always have my operations at the Harbeck Clinic." I was praised for that tidbit, and could not run fast enough to Breezy Lodge with it.

I knew what the medical words meant, for I had begun to learn Greek at school—Ladies Greek, as Elizabeth Barrett Browning called it, "without any accents". My growing knowledge served me well with regard to words spoken in lowered tones. "My operations! How Ralph Townsend will adore that one!" Miss Alliot said.

A Townsend now stepped forward from the general family group. Miss Martin stopped laughing. I was so sharp for my years that I thought she gave herself away by doing so, that she should have let her laughter die away gradually. In that slice of a moment she had made clear her sudden worry about Ralph Townsend. Knowing as I did then so much about human beings, I was sure she had been meant to.

Poor Miss Martin, my friend, mentor, church-going

companion, mild, kind and sincere—I simply used her as a stepping-stone to Miss Alliot.

I never called them by their first names, and have had to pause a little to remember them. Dorothea Alliot and Edith Martin. 'Dorothea' had a fine ring of authority about it. Of course, I had the Greek meaning of that, too, but I knew that Miss Alliot was the giver herself—of the presents and the punishments.

My mother liked playing croquet and cards, and did both a great deal at St Margaret's. I liked going across the orchard to Breezy Lodge. There, both cards and croquet, were despised. We sat on the verandah (or, in winter, round an oil-stove which threw up petal patterns on the ceiling) and we talked—a game particularly suited to three people. Miss Alliot always won.

Where to find such drowsy peace in England now is hard to discover. Summer after summer through my early teens, the sun shone, bringing up the smell of thyme and marjoram from the earth—the melting tar along the lane and, later, of rotting apples. The croquet balls clicked against one another on the lawn, and voices sounded lazy and far-away. There were droughts, when we were on our honour to be careful with the water. No water was laid on at Breezy Lodge, and it had to be carried from the house. I took this duty from Miss Martin, and several times a day stumbled through the long grass and buttercups, the water swinging in a pail, or slopping out of a jug. As I went, I disturbed clouds of tiny blue butterflies, once a grass snake.

Any excuse to get to Breezy Lodge. My mother told me not to intrude, and I was offended by the word. She was even a little frosty about my two friends. If for some reason they were not there when we ourselves arrived on holiday I was in despair, and she knew it and lost patience.

In the school term I wrote to them and Miss Martin was the one who replied. They shared a flat in London, and a visit to it was spoken of, but did not come about. I used my imagination instead, building it up from little scraps as a bird builds a nest. I was able to furnish it in unstained oak and hand-woven rugs and curtains. All about would be jars of the beech-leaves and grasses and berries they took back with them from the country. From their windows could be seen, through the branches of a monkey-puzzle tree, the roofs of the school—Queen's—from which they returned each evening.

That was their life on their own where I could not intrude, as my mother would have put it. They had another life of their own in which I felt aggrieved at not partici-pating: but, I was not invited to. After supper at St Margaret's, they returned to Breezy Lodge, and did not ask me to go with them. Games of solo whist were begun in the drawing-room, and I sat and read listlessly, hearing the clock tick and the maddening mystifying card-words —"Misère" "Abundance"—or "going a bundle," "prop and cop", and "Misère Ouverte" (which seemed to cause a little stir). I pitied them and their boring games, and I pitied myself and my boring book—imposed holiday reading, usually Sir Walter Scott, whom I loathed. I pecked at it disspiritedly and looked about the room for distraction.

Miss Louie and Miss Beatrice enjoyed their whist, as they enjoyed their croquet. They really were hostesses. We paid a little—astonishingly little—but it did not alter the fact that we were truly guests, and they entertained us believing so.

"Ho . . . ho . . . hum . . . hum," murmured a voice, fanning out a newly-dealt hand, someone playing for time. "H'm, h'm, now let me see." There were relaxed intervals when cards were being shuffled and cut, and the players leaned back and had a little desultory conversation, though nothing amounting to much. On warm nights, as it grew later, through the open windows moths came to plunge and lurch about the lamps.

Becoming more and more restless, I might go out and wander about the garden, looking for glow-worms and glancing at the light from Breezy Lodge shining through the orchard boughs.

On other evenings, after Miss Beatrice had lit the lamps, Mrs Mayes, one of the regular guests, might give a Shakespeare recital. She had once had some connection with the stage and had known Sir Henry Ainley. She had often heard his words for him, she told us, and perhaps, in consequence of that, had whole scenes by heart. She was ageing wonderfully—that is, hardly at all. Some of the blonde was fading from her silvery-blonde hair, but her skin was still wild-rose, and her voice held its great range. But most of all, we marvelled at how she remembered her lines. I recall most vividly the Balcony Scene from *Romeo and Juliet*. Mrs Mayes sat at one end of a velvet-covered *chaise-longue*. When she looped her pearls over her fingers, then clasped them to her bosom, she was

Juliet, and Romeo when she held out her arms, imploringly (the rope of pearls swinging free). Always she changed
into what, in some circles, was then called semi-evening
dress, and rather old-fashioned dresses they were, with
bead embroidery and loose panels hanging from the waist.
Once, I imagined, she would have worn such dresses
before tea, and have changed again later into something
even more splendid. She had lived through grander days:
now, was serenely widowed.

Only Mrs Price did not marvel at her. I overheard her
say to my mother, "She must be forever in the limelight,
and I for one am sick and tired, *sick* and *tired*, of Henry
Ainley. I'm afraid I don't call actors 'Sir'. I'm like that."
And my mother blushed, but said nothing.

Miss Alliot and Miss Martin were often invited to stay
for these recitals; but Miss Alliot always declined.

"One is embarrassed, being recited *at*," she explained
to me. "One doesn't know where to look."

I always looked at Mrs Mayes and admired the way she
did her hair, and wondered if the pearls were real. There
may have been a little animosity between the two women.
I remember Mrs Mayes joining in praise of Miss Alliot one
day, saying, "Yes, she is like a well-bred race-horse," and
I felt that she said this only because she could not say that
she was like a horse.

Mrs Price, rather out of it after supper, because of Mrs
Mayes, and not being able to get the hang of solo whist,
would sulkily turn the pages of the *Illustrated London
News*, and try to start conversations between scenes or
games.

"*Do* look at *this*." She would pass round her magazine,

pointing out something or other. Or she would tiptoe upstairs to see if Muriel slept, and come back to report. Once she said, *à propos* nothing, as cards were being re-dealt, "Now who can clasp their ankles with their fingers? Like *that*—with no gaps." Some of the ladies dutifully tried, but only Mrs Price could do it. She shrugged and laughed. "Only a bit of fun," she said, "but they do say that's the right proportion. Wrists, too, that's easier, though." But they were all at cards again.

One morning, we were sitting on the lawn and my mother was stringing red-currants through the tines of a silver fork into a pudding-basin. Guests often helped in these ways. Mrs Price came out from the house carrying a framed photograph of a bride and bridegroom—her son, Derek, and daughter-in-law, Gloria. We had heard of them.

"You don't look old enough," my mother said, "to have a son that age." She had said it before. She always liked to make people happy. Mrs Price kept hold of the photograph, because of my mother's stained fingers, and she pointed out details such as Gloria's veil and Derek's smile and the tuberoses in the bouquet. "Derek gave her a gold locket, but it hasn't come out very clearly. Old enough! You are trying to flatter me. Why my husband and I had our silver wedding last October. Muriel was our little after-thought."

I popped a string of currants into my mouth and sauntered off. As soon as I was out of sight, I sped. All across the orchard, I murmured the words with smiling lips.

The door of Breezy Lodge stood open to the verandah. I called through it, "Muriel was their little after-thought."

Miss Martin was crying. From the bedroom came a muffled sobbing. At once, I knew that it was she, never could be Miss Alliot. Miss Alliot, in fact, walked out of the bedroom and shut the door.

"What is wrong?" I asked stupidly.

Miss Alliot gave a vexed shake of her head and took her walking-stick from its corner. She was wearing a dress with a pattern of large poppies, and cut-out poppies from the same material were appliquéd to her straw hat. She was going for a walk, and I went with her, and she told me that Miss Martin had fits of nervous hysteria. For no reason. The only thing to be done about them was to leave her alone until she recovered.

We went down through the Cherry Orchard and the scents and the butterflies were part of an enchanted world. I thought that I was completely happy. I so rarely had Miss Alliot's undivided attention. She talked of the Town-sends, and I listened as if to the holy intimations of a saint.

"I thought you were lost," my mother said when I returned.

Miss Alliot always wore a hat at luncheon (that annoyed Mrs Price). She sat opposite me and seemed in a very good humour, taking trouble to amuse us all, but with an occasional allusion and smile for me alone. "Miss Martin has one of her headaches," she explained. By this time I was sure that this was true.

The holidays were going by, and I had got nowhere with *Quentin Durward*. Miss Martin recovered from her nervous hysteria, but was subdued.

Miss Alliot departed for Northumberland, wearing autumn tweeds. Miss Martin stayed on alone at Breezy Lodge, and distempered the walls primrose, and I helped her. Mrs Price and Muriel left at last, and a German governess with her two little London pupils arrived for a breath of fresh air. My mother and Mrs Mayes strolled about the garden. Together they did the flowers, to help Miss Louie, or sat together in the sunshine with their *petit point*.

Miss Martin and I painted away, and we talked of Miss Alliot and how wonderful she was. It was like a little separate holiday for me, a rest. I did not try to adjust myself to Miss Martin, or strive, or rehearse. In a way, I think she was having a well-earned rest herself; but then I believed that she was jealous of Northumberland and would have liked some Townsends of her own to retaliate with. Now I know she only wanted Miss Alliot.

Miss Martin was conscientious; she even tried to take me through *Quentin Durward*.

She seemed to be concerned about my butterfly mind, its skimming over things, not stopping to understand. I felt that knowing things ought to 'come' to me, and if it did not, it was too bad. I believed in instinct and intuition and inspiration—all labour-saving things.

Miss Martin, who taught English (my subject, I felt), approached the matter coldly. She tried to teach me the logic of it—grammar. But I thought 'ear' would somehow teach me that. Painless learning I wanted, or none at all. She would not give up. She was the one who was fond of me.

We returned from our holiday, and I went back to school. I was moved up—by the skin of my teeth, I am sure—to a higher form. I remained with my friends. Some of those had been abroad for the holidays, but I did not envy them.

Miss Martin wrote to enquire how I had got on in the *Quentin Durward* test, and I replied that as I could not answer one question, I had written a general description of Scottish scenery. She said that it would avail me nothing, and it did not. I had never been to Scotland, anyway. Of Miss Alliot I only heard. She was busy producing the school play—*A Tale of Two Cities*. Someone called Rosella Byng-Williams was very good as Sidney Carton, and I took against her at once. "I think Dorothea has made quite a discovery," Miss Martin wrote—but I fancied that her pen was pushed along with difficulty, and that she was due for one of her headaches.

Those three 'i's'—instinct, intuition, inspiration—in which I pinned my faith were more useful in learning about people than logic could be. Capricious approach to capricious subject.

Looking back, I see that my mother was far more attractive, lovable, than any of the ladies I describe; but there it was—she was my mother.

Towards the end of that term, I learned of a new thing, that Miss Alliot was to spend Christmas with the Townsends. This had never been done before: there had been simply the early autumn visit—it seemed that it had been for the sake of an old family friendship, a one-sided one, I sharply guessed. Now, what had seemed to be a yearly courtesy, became something rather more for conjecture.

Miss Martin wrote that she would go to Breezy Lodge alone, and pretend that Christmas wasn't happening—as lonely people strive to. I imagined her carrying pails of cold water through the wet, long grasses of the orchard, rubbing her chilblains before the oil-stove. I began to love her as if she were a child.

My mother was a little flustered by my idea of having Miss Martin to stay with us for Christmas. I desired it intensely, having reached a point where the two of us, my mother and I alone, a Christmas done just for me, was agonising. What my mother thought of Miss Martin I shall never know now, but I have a feeling that school-mistresses rather put her off. She expected them all to be what many of them in those days were—opinionated, narrow-minded, set in their ways. She had never tried to get to know Miss Martin. No one ever did.

She came. At the last moment before her arrival I panicked. It was not Miss Alliot coming, but Miss Alliot would hear all about the visit. Our house was in a terrace (crumbling). There was nothing, I now saw, to commend it to Miss Martin except, perhaps, water from the main and a coal fire.

After the first nervousness, though, we had a cosy time. We sat round the fire and ate chinese figs and sipped ginger wine and played paper games which Miss Martin could not manage to lose. We sometimes wondered about the Townsends and I imagined a sort of Royal-Family-at-Sandringham Christmas with a giant tree and a servants' ball, and Miss Alliot taking the floor in the arms of Ralph Townsend—but then my imagination failed, the picture faded: I could not imagine Miss Alliot in the arms of any man.

After Christmas, Miss Martin left and then I went back to school. I was too single-minded in my devotion to Miss Alliot to do much work there, or bother about anybody else. My infatuation was fed by her absence, and everything beautiful was wasted if it was not seen in her company.

The Christmas invitation bore glorious fruit. As a return, Miss Martin wrote to ask me to stay at Breezy Lodge for my half-term holiday. Perfect happiness invaded me, remembered clearly to this day. Then, after a while of walking on air, the bliss dissolved. Nothing in the invitation, I now realised, had been said of Miss Alliot. Perhaps she was off to Northumberland again, and I was to keep Miss Martin company in her stead. I tried to reason with myself that even that would be better than nothing, but I stayed sick with apprehension.

At the end of the bus-ride there on a Saturday morning, I was almost too afraid to cross the orchard. I feared my own disappointment as if it were something I must protect myself and—incidentally Miss Martin—from. I seemed to become two people—the one who tapped jauntily on the door, and the other who stood ready to ward off the worst. Which did not happen. Miss Alliot herself opened the door.

She was wearing one of her bandeaux and several ropes of beads and had a rather gypsy air about her. "The child has arrived," she called back into the room. Miss Martin sat by the stove mending stockings—an occupation of those days. They were Miss Alliot's stockings—rather thick and biscuit-coloured.

We went over to St Margaret's for lunch and walked to the Echo afterwards returning with branches of catkins and budding twigs. Miss Alliot had a long, loping stride. She hit about at nettles with her stick, the fringed tongues of her brogues flapped—she had long, narrow feet, and trouble with high insteps, she complained. The bandeau was replaced by a stitched felt hat in which was stuck the eye-part of a peacock's feather. Bad luck, said Miss M. Bosh, said Miss A.

We had supper at Breezy Lodge, for Miss Alliot's latest craze was for making goulash, and a great pot of it was to be consumed during the weekend. Afterwards, Miss Martin knitted—a jersey of complicated Fair Isle pattern for Miss Alliot. She sat in a little perplexed world of her own, entangled by coloured wools, her head bent over the instructions.

Miss Alliot turned her attention to me. What was my favourite line of poetry, what would I do if I were suddenly given a thousand pounds, would I rather visit Rome or Athens or New York, which should I hate most—being deaf or blind; hanged or drowned; are cats not better than dogs, and wild-flowers more beautiful than garden ones, and Emily Brontë streets ahead of Charlotte? And so on. It was heady stuff to me. No one before had been interested in my opinions. Miss Martin knitted on. Occasionally, she was included in the questions, and always appeared to give the wrong answer.

I slept in their bedroom, on a camp-bed borrowed from

St Margaret's. (And how was I ever going to be satisfied with staying *there* again? I wondered.)

Miss Alliot bagged (as she put it) the bathroom first, and was already in bed by the time I returned from what was really only a ewer of water and an Elsan. She was wearing black silk pyjamas with D.D.A. embroidered on a pocket. I bitterly regretted my pink nightgown, of which I had until then been proud. I had hastily brushed my teeth and passed a wet flannel over my face in eagerness to get back to her company and, I hoped, carry on with the entrancing subject of my likes and dislikes.

I began to undress. "People are kind to the blind, and impatient with the deaf," I began, as if there had been no break in the conversation. "You are so right," Miss Alliot said. "And people matter most."

"But if you couldn't see . . . well, this orchard in spring," Miss Martin put in. It was foolish of her to do so. "You've already seen it," Miss Alliot pointed out. "Why this desire to go on repeating your experiences?"

Miss Martin threw in the Parthenon, which she had *not* seen, and hoped to.

"Still people matter most," Miss Alliot insisted. "To be cut off from them is worse than to be cut off from the Acropolis."

She propped herself up in bed and with open curiosity watched me undress. For the first time in my life I realised what dreadful things I wore beneath my dress—lockknit petticoat, baggy school bloomers, vest with Cash's name tape, garters of stringy elastic tied in knots, not sewn. My mother had been right . . . I should have sewn them. Then, for some reason, I turned my back to Miss Alliot and put on my nightgown. I need not have bothered, for Miss Martin was there between us in a flash, standing before Miss Alliot with Ovaltine.

On the next day—Sunday—I renounced my religion. My doubts made it impossible for me to go to church, so Miss Martin went alone. She went rather miserably, I was forced to notice. I can scarcely believe that any deity could have been interested in my lack of devotion, but it was as if, somewhere, there was one who was. Freak weather had set in and, although spring had not yet begun, the sun was so warm that Miss Alliot took a deck-chair and a blanket and sat on the verandah and went fast asleep until long after Miss Martin had returned. (She *needed* a great deal of sleep, she always said.) I pottered about and fretted at this waste of time. I almost desired my faith again. I waited for Miss Martin to come back, and, seeing her, ran out and held a finger to my lips, as if Miss Alliot were royalty, or a baby. Miss Martin nodded and came on stealthily.

It was before the end of the summer term that I had the dreadful letter from Miss Martin. Miss Alliot—hadn't we both feared it?—was engaged to be married to Ralph Townsend. Of course, that put paid to my examinations. In the event of more serious matters, I scrawled off anything that came into my head. As for questions, I wanted to answer them only if they were asked by Miss Alliot, and they must be personal, not factual. As usual, if I didn't know what I was asked in the examination paper, I did a piece about something else. I imagined some *rapport* being made, and that was what I wanted from life.

Miss Martin's letter was taut and unrevealing. She stated the facts—the date, the place. An early autumn wedding it was to be, in Northumberland, as Miss Alliot had now no family of her own. I had never supposed that she had. At the beginning of a voyage, a liner needs some small tugs to help it on its way, but they are soon dispensed with.

Before the wedding, there were the summer holidays, and the removal of their things from Breezy Lodge, for Miss Martin had no heart, she said, to keep it on alone.

During that last holiday, Miss Martin's face was terrible. It seemed to be fading, like an old, old photograph. Miss Alliot, who was not inclined to jewelry ("Would you prefer diamonds to Rembrandts?" once she had asked me), had taken off her father's signet ring and put in its place a half hoop of diamonds. Quite incongruous, I thought.

I was weeks older. Time was racing ahead for me. A boy called Jamie was staying at St. Margaret's with his parents. After supper, while Mrs Mayes's recitals were going on, or the solo whist, he and I sat outside the drawing-room on the stairs, and he told me blood-chilling stories, which I have since read in Edgar Allan Poe.

Whenever Jamie saw Miss Alliot, he began to hum a song of those days—"Horsy, keep your tail up." My mother thought he was a bad influence, and so another frost set in.

Sometimes—not often, though—I went to Breezy Lodge. The Fair Isle sweater was put aside. Miss Martin's having diminished, diminished everything, including Miss

Alliot. Nothing was going on there, no goulash, no darning, no gathering of branches.

"Yes, she's got a face like a horse," Jamie said again and again.

And I said nothing.

"But he's *old*." Miss Martin moved her hands about in her lap, regretted her words, fell silent.

"Old? How old?" I asked.

"He's seventy."

I had known that Miss Alliot was doing something dreadfully, dangerously wrong. She could not be in love with Ralph Townsend; but with the Townsends entire.

On the day they left, I went to Breezy Lodge to say goodbye. It looked squalid, with the packing done—something horribly shabby, ramshackle about it.

Later, I went with Jamie to the Echo and we shouted one another's names across the valley. His name came back very clearly. When we returned, Miss Alliot and Miss Martin had gone forever.

Miss Alliot was married in September. Miss Martin tried sharing her London flat with someone else, another schoolmistress. I wrote to her once, and she replied.

Towards Christmas my mother had a letter from Miss Louie to say that she had heard Miss Martin was dead— "by her own hand," she wrote, in her shaky handwriting.

"I am HORRIFIED," I informed my diary that night—the five-year diary that was full of old sayings of Miss Alliot, and descriptions of her clothes.

I have quite forgotten what Jamie looked like—but I can still see Miss Alliot clearly, her head back, looking down her nose, her mouth contemptuous, and poor Miss Martin's sad, scribbly face.

The Fly-paper

ON Wednesdays, after school, Sylvia took the bus
to the outskirts of the nearest town for her music
lesson. Because of her docile manner, she did not complain
of the misery she suffered in Miss Harrison's darkened
parlour, sitting at the old-fashioned upright piano with its
brass candlesticks and loose, yellowed keys. In the highest
register there was not the faintest tinkle of a note, only the
hollow sound of the key being banged down. Although
that distant octave was out of her range, Sylvia sometimes
pressed down one of its notes, listening mutely to Miss
Harrison's exasperated railings about her—Sylvia's—lack
of aptitude, or even concentration. The room was darkened in winter by a large fir-tree pressing against—in
windy weather tapping against—the window, and in
summer even more so by holland blinds, half-drawn to
preserve the threadbare carpet. To add to all the other
miseries, Sylvia had to peer short-sightedly at the music-
book, her glance going up and down between it and the
keyboard, losing her place, looking hunted, her lips pursed.

It was now the season of the drawn blinds, and she
waited in the lane at the bus-stop, feeling hot in her winter
coat, which her grandmother insisted on her wearing, just
as she insisted on the music lessons. The lane buzzed
in the heat of the late afternoon—with bees in the
clover, and flies going crazy over some cow-pats on the
road.

Since her mother's death, Sylvia had grown glum and

sullen. She was a plain child, plump, mature for her eleven years. Her greasy hair was fastened back by a pink plastic slide; her tweed coat, of which, last winter, she had been rather proud, had cuffs and collar of mock ocelot. She carried, beside her music case, a shabby handbag, once her mother's.

The bus seemed to tremble and jingle as it came slowly down the road. She climbed on, and sat down on the long seat inside the door, where a little air might reach her.

On the other long seat opposite her, was a very tall man; quite old, she supposed, for his hair was carefully arranged over his bald skull. He stared at her. She puffed with the heat and then, to avoid his glance, she slewed round a little to look over her shoulder at the dusty hedges—the leaves all in late summer darkness. She was sure that he was wondering why she wore a winter's coat on such a day, and she unbuttoned it and flapped it a little to air her armpits. The weather had a threat of change in it, her grandmother had said, and her cotton dress was too short. It had already been let down and had a false hem, which she now tried to draw down over her thighs.

"Yes, it is very warm," the man opposite her suddenly said, as if agreeing with someone else's remark.

She turned in surprise, and her face reddened, but she said nothing.

After a while, she began to wonder if it would be worth getting off at the fare-stage before the end of her journey and walk the rest of the way. Then she could spend the money on a lolly. She had to waste half-an-hour before her lesson, and must wander about somewhere to pass the time. It would be better to be wandering about with a lolly to suck. Her grandmother did not allow her to eat sweets —bathing the teeth in acid, she said it was.

"I believe I have seen you before," the man opposite said. "Either wending your way to or from a music-lesson, I imagine." He looked knowingly at her music-case.

"To," she said sullenly.

"A budding Myra Hess," he went on. "I take it that you play the piano, as you seem to have no instrument secreted about your person."

She did not know what he meant, and stared out of the window, frowning, feeling so hot and anguished.

"And what is your name?" he asked. "We shall have to keep it in mind for the future when you are famous."

"Sylvia Wilkinson," she said under her breath.

"Not bad. Not bad, Sylvia. No doubt one day I shall boast that I met the great Sylvia Wilkinson on a bus one summer's afternoon. Name-dropping, you know. A harmless foible of the humble."

He was very neat and natty, but his reedy voice had a nervous tremor. All this time, he had held an unlighted cigarette in his hand, and gestured with it, but made no attempt to find matches.

"I expect at school you sing the beautiful song, 'Who is Sylvia?' Do you?"

She shook her head, without looking at him and, to her horror, he began to sing, quaveringly, "Who is Sylvia? What is she-he?"

A woman sitting a little farther down the bus, turned and looked at him sharply.

He's mad, Sylvia decided. She was embarrassed, but not nervous, not nervous at all, here in the bus with other people, in spite of all her grandmother had said about not getting into conversations with strangers.

He went on singing, wagging his cigarette in time.

The woman turned again and gave him a longer stare. She was homely-looking, Sylvia decided—in spite of fair hair going very dark at the roots. She had a comfortable, protective manner, as if she were keeping an eye on the situation for Sylvia's sake.

Suddenly, he broke off his singing and returned her stare. "I take it, Madam," he said, "that you do not appreciate my singing."

"I should think it's hardly the place," she said shortly. "That's all," and turned her head away.

"Hardly the place!" he said, in a low voice, as if to himself, and with feigned amazement. "On a fair summer's afternoon, while we bowl merrily along the lanes. Hardly the place—to express one's joy of living! I am sorry," he said to Sylvia, in a louder voice. "I had not realised we were going to a funeral."

Thankfully, she saw that they were coming nearer to the outskirts of the town. It was not a large town, and its outskirts were quiet.

"I hope you don't mind me chatting to you," the man said to Sylvia. "I am fond of children. I am known as being *good* with them. Well known for that. I treat them on my own level, as one should."

Sylvia stared—almost glared—out of the window, twisted round in her seat, her head aching with the stillness of her eyes.

It was flat country, intersected by canals. On the skyline, were the clustered chimneys of a brick-works. The only movement out there was the faintest shimmering of heat.

She was filled by misery; for there seemed nothing in her life now but acquiescence to hated things, and her grandmother's old ways setting her apart from other children. Nothing she did was what she wanted to do—school-going, church-going, now this terrible music lesson ahead of her. Since her mother's death, her life had taken a sharp turn for the worse, and she could not see how it would ever be any better. She had no faith in freeing herself from it, even when she was grown-up.

A wasp zigzagged across her and settled on the front of her coat. She was obliged to turn. She sat rigid, her head held back, her chin tucked in, afraid to make a movement.

"Allow me!" The awful man opposite had reached across the bus, and flapped a crumpled handkerchief at her. The wasp began to fuss furiously, darting about her face.

"We'll soon settle you, you little pest," the man said, making matters worse.

The bus-conductor came between them. He stood carefully still for a moment, and then decisively clapped his hands together, and the wasp fell dead to the ground.

"Thank you," Sylvia said to him, but not to the other.

They were passing bungalows now, newly-built, and with unmade gardens. Looking directly ahead of her, Sylvia got up, and went to the platform of the bus, standing there in a slight breeze, ready for the stopping-place.

Beyond the bus-shelter, she knew that there was a little general shop. She would comfort herself with a bright red lolly on a stick. She crossed the road and stood looking in the window, at jars of boiled sweets, and packets of detergents and breakfast cereals. There was a notice about ice-creams, but she had not enough money.

She turned to go into the empty, silent shop when the now familiar and dreaded voice came from beside her. "Would you care to partake of an ice, this hot afternoon?"

He stood between her and the shop, and the embarrassment she had suffered on the bus gave way to terror.

"An ice?" he repeated, holding his head on one side, looking at her imploringly.

She thought that if she said 'yes', she could at least get inside the shop. Someone must be there to serve, someone whose protection she might depend upon. Those words of warning from her grandmother came into her head, cautionary tales, dark with unpleasant hints.

Before she could move, or reply, she felt a hand lightly but firmly touch her shoulder. It was the glaring woman from the bus, she was relieved to see.

"Haven't you ever been told not to talk to strangers?" she asked Sylvia, quite sharply, but with calm common sense in her brusqueness. "*You'd* better be careful," she said to the man menacingly. "Now come along, child, and let this be a lesson to you. Which way were you going?"

Sylvia nodded ahead.

"Well, best foot forward, and keep going. And *you*, my man, can kindly step in a different direction, or I'll find a policeman."

At this last word, Sylvia turned to go, feeling flustered, but important.

"You should *never*," the woman began, going along

beside her. "There's some funny people about these days. Doesn't your mother warn you?"

"She's dead."

"Oh, well, I'm sorry about that. My God, it's warm." She pulled her dress away from her bosom, fanning it. She had a shopping-basket full of comforting, homely groceries, and Sylvia looked into it, as she walked beside her.

"Wednesday's always my day," the woman said. "Early-closing here, so I take the bus up to Horseley. I have a relative who has the little general store there. It makes a change, but not in this heat."

She rambled on about her uninteresting affairs. Once, Sylvia glanced back, and could see the man still standing there, gazing after them.

"I shouldn't turn round," the woman said. "Which road did you say?"

Sylvia hadn't, but now did so.

"Well, you can come my way. That would be better, and there's nothing much in it. Along by the gravel-pits. I'll have a quick look round before we turn the corner."

When she did so, she said that she thought they were being followed, at a distance. "Oh, it's disgraceful," she said. "And with all the things you read in the papers. You can't be too careful, and you'll have to remember that in the future. I'm not sure I ought not to inform the police."

Along this road, there were disused gravel-pits, and chicory and convolvulus. Rusty sorrel and rustier tin-cans gave the place a derelict air. On the other side, there were allotments, and ramshackle tool-sheds among dark nettles.

"It runs into Hamilton Road," the woman explained.

"But I don't have to be there for another half-hour," Sylvia said nervously. She could imagine Miss Harrison's face if she turned up on the doorstep all that much too soon, in the middle of a lesson with the bright-looking girl she had often met leaving.

"I'm going to give you a nice cup of tea, and make sure you're all right. Don't you worry."

Thankfully, she turned in at the gate of a little red brick house at the edge of the waste land. It was ugly, but very neat, and surrounded by hollyhocks. The beautifully shining windows were draped with frilly, looped-up curtains, with plastic flowers arranged between them.

Sylvia followed the woman down a side path to the back door, trying to push her worries from her mind. She was all right this time, but what of all the future Wednesdays, she wondered—with their perilous journeys to be made alone.

She stood in the kitchen and looked about her. It was clean and cool there. A budgerigar hopped in a cage. Rather listlessly, but not knowing what else to do, she went to it and ran her finger-nail along the wires.

"There's my baby boy, my little Joey," the woman said in a sing-song, automatic way, as she held the kettle under the tap. "You'll feel better when you've had a cup of tea," she added, now supposedly addressing Sylvia.

"It's very kind of you."

"Any woman would do the same. There's a packet of Oval Marie in my basket, if you'd like to open it and put them on this plate."

Sylvia was glad to do something. She arranged the biscuits carefully on the rose-patterned plate. "It's very nice here," she said. Her grandmother's house was so dark and cluttered; Miss Harrison's even more so. Both smelt stuffy, of thick curtains and old furniture. She did not go into many houses, for she was so seldom invited anywhere. She was a dull girl, whom nobody liked very much, and she knew it.

"I must have everything sweet and fresh," the woman said complacently.

The kettle began to sing.

I've still got to get home, Sylvia thought in a panic. She stared up at a fly-paper hanging in the window—the only disconcerting thing in the room. Some of the flies were still half alive, and striving hopelessly to free themselves. But they were caught forever.

She heard footsteps on the path, and listened in surprise; but the woman did not seem to hear, or lift her head. She was spooning tea from the caddy into the teapot.

"Just in time, Herbert," she called out.

Sylvia turned round as the door opened. With astonished horror, she saw the man from the bus step confidently into the kitchen.

"Well done, Mabel!" he said, closing the door behind him. "Don't forget one for the pot." He smiled, smoothing his hands together, surveying the room.

Sylvia spun round questioningly to the woman, who was now bringing the teapot to the table, and she noticed for the first time that there were three cups and saucers laid there.

"Well, sit down, do," the woman said, a little impatiently. "It's all ready."

Crêpes Flambées

HARRY and Rose, returning to Mahmoud Souk, found it a great deal changed. Along the sea road there were neat beds of Mesembrianthemum. There were lamp-standards, too; branches of globes, in the Parisian manner. Four years before, there had been only a stretch of stony sand, a low sea wall, an unmade road. Now new buildings were glittering along the shore—a hospital, a cinema, a second hotel.

Until they had reached the town, nothing in this country seemed to have changed—not in the last four years, nor in the last four thousand. Veiled women walked beside donkeys that were laden with water-pots or the trimmings of olive trees; old men, hooded against the wind, stood amongst grazing sheep. They were all like extras in some vast film of Bible times.

Rose remembered the Arab habit of stillness—how what had seemed to be a large boulder amongst the scrub would, after a quarter of an hour, stir slightly. Rather sinister, she found it—especially when the figures leaned, stiff as corpses, against a wall, perhaps begging, or just *being*.

Rose and Harry had rattled along the roads in their car hired from Tunis, driving south, as they had done four years before on their honeymoon. On the other side of the bay, they could see, for a long time before they reached it, the whiteness of Mahmoud Souk. Both were excited and apprehensive. To return some might think a mistake, but they had always intended to; indeed, had promised Habib and the others that they would—those friends they had made in Habib's café: Mustapha, the thin and the fat Mohameds, Le Nègre—and other habitués whose names they had forgotten.

They drew up at the hotel right by the sandy shore, and the porter ran out to fetch their cases—a different porter, but this small disappointment could be brushed aside in the excitement of arriving.

The hotel, at least, was familiar. It had its own especial echo and smell—an echo from so much polished stone and tiles, and the smell of Tunisian cooking striving to be European.

"We'll go later, don't you think?" Harry asked Rose. He crossed the bedroom to the window, unwound the shutters and squinted down in the direction of Habib's café, though knowing that it was just out of sight.

Rose knew what he meant. They were so much alike that it was quite extraordinary. Their friends back home in London had discovered that they could confide in them both at the same time, without embarrassment. It was like confiding in one person.

They unpacked happily, looking forward to the drink later, and the welcome they would have in the little garden in front of Habib's café, facing the sea and the mimosa trees.

"You remember your birthday?" Rose said to Harry, as she had said so many times.

It stood apart from all the other birthdays in England. After dinner, there had been a party in the café. One or two English people from the hotel had looked in, had come and gone; but Harry had gone on for ever, drinking beer and bouka, anything that came to hand. And then, suddenly, Habib had stood up on a chair and declared it midnight and not Harry's birthday any more, but his own. They made more speeches to one another; they were comrades, brothers, born almost on the same day.

They always spoke in French, and Rose found it easier to understand than the French that French people speak.

She and Harry were still remembering that beautiful birthday, when they walked along the sea-road towards the café. *La Sirène* it was called. On the edge of the pavement, there had stood a sign cut out of thin wood—a blue and green mermaid carrying a faded list of prices.

"Perhaps they won't remember us," Rose said. She felt rather shy and nervous.

"They will," said Harry.

He had sent a photograph to them—of Rose and the others standing by the painted mermaid—and he could imagine this pinned up in the bar: rather curled and discoloured it may be by now, but there it would be; for photographs were hard to come by, and prized.

"It isn't there," Rose said, as they turned the curve of the sea-road. She meant the mermaid.

"Perhaps it fell to pieces, or got blown away," Harry said; but their pace had quickened from anxiety.

La Sirène was deserted. In fact, it no longer was *La Sirène*, but a dark shell, sliding into decay. The benches and tables were gone from the garden, and old pieces of paper had been blown against the front door.

Rose and Harry pushed open the gate, and walked up the short path. Grit and sand and fluff from the mimosa trees swirled round the garden. They peered through the window-grilles into the dim, depressing interior. There was nothing left but marks upon the bare walls and dusty floor. Marks where the bar had stood, and on the walls where shelves and notices had hung, and the big coloured picture of President Bourguiba.

They walked quite sadly away, and went back to the hotel for their drink, sitting in silence for once, feeling let down.

"I wonder what happened . . ." Rose said. "I wish I knew."

"We need not stay here," Harry said; for he knew the magic of Mahmoud Souk was gone. "We could drive south—that would be new ground to us."

"It's such a pity. So different from what I'd imagined."

"After all, just because one or two Arabs in a café . . ."

"You know it isn't only that . . . although they made us seem less like strangers."

"It was really our stake in the country as a whole."

"I suppose . . . yes, let's go. This bar is saddening."

There was no one else there. Outside, on the terrace, a party of Germans lay spread out on *chaises-longues* exposed to the last of the day's sun.

Next morning, their gaiety was revived by the trembling brightness of the air, and orange-juice and coffee on the terrace. The Germans were already sunbathing, stirring only to shift another part of their bodies into the sun, as if they were revolving methodically upon spits. At seven o'clock, Rose had been wakened by the voices outside—"*'Morgen!*" "*'Morgen!*" they had shouted to one another—two men—as they spread about their towels and books and lotions, bagging the best places for the day. They had taken over the hotel and this, at dinner the evening before, had made Rose and Harry feel waifish and ignored, and missing Habib and the rest more than ever.

This morning, after breakfast, stepping off the sheltered terrace, they felt the edge of a strong wind. A veil of sand was racing along the shore. Grit swirled about the building sites, the big rubble-covered spaces where once crumbling hovels had stood, and soon hotels and blocks of flats and other cafés than Habib's would rise.

"The Germans have the best of it," Harry grumbled. "Organised as ever."

The wind made them both feel inharmonious, irritable.

When they came to the high walls of the *medina*, they went inside with relief. Here it was sheltered, and the air smelt spicy and of burning charcoal. They wandered in the *souk*, Rose either feasting, or averting, her eyes— exclaiming about the heaps of young vegetables, or flinching at the sight of a furry, bloody sheep's head hanging over a butcher's stall.

The narrow alleys buzzed with children. Little girls in blue overalls wearing ear-rings were inclined to be cheeky. "*Bonjour, madame!*" they called to Rose, over their shoulders, just after they had passed by.

It became a bore. The children grew bolder.

"Don't take any notice," Harry implored.

She always made the mistake of encouraging them, of smiling and waving and replying; so that they were usually followed by a band of youngsters, even toddlers, with hands outstretched for money, or with wilting flowers for sale. Boys were only too ready with guide-like information about *souks* and mosques. They jostled with one another for the job, and by the time Rose and Harry had reached the street of the carpet-makers, one slim, curious boy, by some means had outwitted the others, and also, by the beauty of his manners, had forced Rose and Harry to succumb.

Courteously, he ushered them into one of the interiors, where they really did not want to go. It was dim and muffled inside and smelled of wool. Just beyond the entrance, sat the Bedouin women, with kohl-rimmed eyes and rouged faces and gaudy rags and tatters, winding the wool, squatting on the floor before revolving frames, babies and little children lying beside them.

"*Passez, passez,*" indicated the young boy, with a graceful movement of his thin and grubby hand. His friends had disappeared, having seen that there was now nothing in it for them.

In the inner rooms, Arab women were working at the looms, knotting and snipping at a great speed, ramming down the tufted wool. Their eyes flew from the looms to the design cards pinned up beside them, but never towards Rose and Harry, whereas the Bedouins, when they passed them again, going out, stared at them mockingly, with their sharp eyes.

Having tipped the guide and refused other delights, Rose and Harry, ignoring his entreaties, strolled on. The alley was hung with skeins of dyed wool. All of the little streets had their own character. They went through the clattering metal-workers' lane into the more leisurely, gossipy street where the barbers' shops were, and the stalls of sickly-looking cakes.

Down two steps from one of the barbers' shops, only half-shaved, ran Habib, wiping soapy foam from his chin with the back of his hand, his old brown coat slung over, slipping from, one shoulder. Hitching up the coat, he shook hands, as if it were yesterday that he had seen them last, not four years ago.

It was Harry he loved; Harry upon whom the true warmth of his welcome fell. Rose knew this. She had always sat meekly by, the one whose French rarely rose to the occasion. A foreign woman was, in any case, an oddity. They broke the rules of Habib's womenfolk. Rose sat unconcernedly in cafés, smoking, drinking hard liquor, with her bare face, bare arms, bare legs. All the same, Habib and his friends had been friendly and respectful to her—live and let live—even if they could not quite admire and love her. She had set a little restraint, which perhaps only Harry's exuberance could have dispelled. If she had not been Harry's wife, none of them would have glanced at her—or only once, in passing. She was, for one thing, for their tastes, too thin.

"She has not changed," Habib said, smiling at her, talking to Harry. "Still so thin."

She could understand his French, if he could not understand hers. She laughed. All her life she had had little intermittent and half-hearted struggles with her weight, always hoping to whittle away (as the fashion magazines put it) a couple of inches from her waist.

Habib had apparently forgotten about the rest of his

shave. He led them triumphantly down to a café by the *medina* gate.

"We looked for *La Sirène* and it was not there," Rose said, having formed the sentence in French before she spoke.

Habib agreed that this was possible; but he looked troubled and guarded. He pursed his lips in a girlish pout and shrugged his shoulders.

Coffee was brought, and he sipped it daintily. He had a round, expressive face and mournful eyes. He looked shabbier than before—but had a touch of flamboyance in the fluorescent lime-green socks, which had 'gone to sleep', as nannies say, above his grey plimsolls.

"I had a good situation offered to me," he said at last with dignity, dropping his eyelids.

La Sirène, it was obvious, had collapsed. To say there had been no capital behind it, was a grand way of saying that it was scarcely solvent. Only when one bottle of *Ricard* had been sold, could Habib afford to slip out to buy another. Until half-way through March the place was closed.

Harry, who seemed unlikely to give offence, enquired about his new job.

"I am chef at the new hotel," Habib replied. He seemed not yet to have decided whether to be proud or ashamed of this. From having been his own master ... le patron ... He shrugged again.

"And what about all our comrades?" asked Harry. "The two Mohameds, Le Nègre, and Mustapha?"

They had all departed—to work in the larger towns. Le Nègre had even gone as far as France.

"And you . . . you are married?" Harry asked.

Habib smiled shyly, and nodded.

"To Fatma?"

They had heard of Fatma before.

Habib nodded again. "Two little children," he said, turning to Rose. That was her province, he felt, although, as it emerged in a minute or two, she had none of her own. He was sorry for Harry about that.

"Boys, or girls, or both?"

"Two girls," he said, smiling bravely.

Harry got up and called for more coffee. As soon as it was served, Habib darted inside the café and came out with a few roasted almonds in a screw of sad old brown paper. He pushed them towards Rose, tapping the table, insisting that she should eat.

"It is like old times," she said.

"The photograph," he said eagerly, turning from one to the other and at last to Rose. "You, me, Mustapha . . ." He waved his hand. "It is hanging on the wall of my new house."

"Where is your house?"

"It is a very fine house, very large. In the country," he added vaguely. He thought about it for a while, then said, "I shall take you there. For a certainty. I shall introduce you to Fatma and the children. I shall cook for you. *La haute cuisine. Crêpes flambées*, you know."

"That will be very nice," Rose said. "Thank you."

"You have a car?" he asked Harry, who nodded.

"Then we shall make many journeys."

"What about your work?"

"On my free day. In the mornings before I go to the

hotel. Perhaps in the afternoons. All the time you are here, I shall not take my *siesta*."

He knew *they* never did, had, from the upper window of *La Sirène*, while yawning, and scratching his chest, and preparing for his sleep, seen them going off, with bathing things, or scrambling on the rocks.

"Now I am afraid I must go to the hotel, to *la haute cuisine*."

"We must dine there one evening, and sample your cooking," Harry said.

"It is superb."

He stood up and shook hands. "This evening at nine o'clock, I shall be in the café next to the new cinema," he said carelessly. He did not invite them to join him and, before they could reply, he had gone, moving swiftly as always, through the *medina* gateway, still only half-shaved.

After dinner at their own hotel, Rose and Harry strolled under the eucalyptus trees, through which a few street-lamps filtered their light, towards the cinema. The wind had, for the time being, dropped, and the air held a romantic stillness.

The barbers' shops, which were everywhere, were still opened, and there was a leisurely coming-and-going in the rubble-strewn streets. Mahmoud Souk was beginning to be as they had remembered it.

At the café by the cinema, men in their brown djellebahs sat at the tables smoking, playing cards and dominoes. There were no Europeans, no women. The Germans had stayed in the hotel lounge, writing their picture-postcards of cobalt skies and camels and palm-trees, and comparing the prices of rugs and copper-work. Dinner had been rather geared to them, with liver dumplings and *sauerkraut*. The old French influence was fading.

"Perhaps Habib's hotel would be better," Rose said, sitting outside the café, her fluffy coat wrapped round her. "To think of *him* becoming a chef! When one remembers the deplorable *couscous*.

They laughed, and then looked round cautiously.

The *couscous* had been a calamity. Habib had invited them as his guests to *La Sirène*. They had sat in a small room at the back, mercifully alone, and the big dish of greasy semolina and hunks of fat mutton and enormous carrots had been set before them. It was cold and daunting. Every time Habib popped his head round the door from serving a customer, they had nodded appreciatively, their mouths full. He went back to report on the pleasure they were having, and sometimes a customer looked in to see for himself. They had plodded on—Rose, especially, in much distress—but had seemed to make no impression upon the great heap on the dish. Then Rose had her clever idea. In her handbag was a folded, plastic rain-hood. Furtively, she opened it—whenever the coast seemed clear —dropped a handful of *couscous* into it.

"All gone," Habib went back at last, triumphantly, to declare.

After that, those hoods were always known to Rose and Harry as *couscous* bags. The idea had been good; but the sequel to it was bad. She had tipped the contents, later, down the lavatory in the hotel, and blocked the drains.

The semolina must have swollen there, as some of it had already swollen inside her.

"The meal in his house," she said, looking round again, and speaking in a low voice, although in English. "This time we shan't be alone . . ."

"He has promised us *la haute cuisine*."

"I *know*," she said doubtfully.

"We'll go to his hotel and try it first," he said.

"Isn't he awfully late?" she suggested.

Harry looked at his watch. "Only half an hour," he said, and ordered another drink.

"It's getting chilly."

"Well, let's go inside."

But she hardly liked to. It seemed very much a man's place in there. Habib might be embarrassed.

When the time came for the next drink, however, she was driven there, shivering. No one took any notice.

It was much later—when they were talking of going back to the hotel—when Habib arrived, coming swiftly on his plimsolled feet. He was smoothly shaven now.

Rather aloof with his acquaintances, he hardly paused to speak to them as he passed their table. He came and shook hands and sat down, leaning forward to talk to them in a both confident and confiding manner.

"So many people asking for *crêpes flambées* at the last moment," he explained importantly.

"You do French cooking always?" Rose asked.

"Every kind; any kind," he replied.

He handed round cigarettes and leaned back, crossing one leg over the other, displaying the fluorescent socks.

"Tomorrow morning, you shall take some photographs,

I think," he said. Photographs had always been of extreme importance to him. "You will take me and Monsieur Harry, if you please," he told Rose, who was not hurt, knowing her place. "If you are able," he added. Then, looking at Harry, he said, "In exchange, I will give you a picture of Madame Bourguiba. In colour."

"Well, that would be splendid. I will also take photographs of Fatma and your children," he promised.

Habib nodded vaguely, as if his family were a thing he had made up, and then forgotten.

"And of your house."

He brightened. "It is a very big house. Quite new. There are beds, cupboards, chairs, everything." He did not know the French for grass-matting, so pointed to some at their feet. "A goat," he went on, "hens, donkey, vines. All you could wish."

"You earn good money then," asked Harry, who could ask anything.

"Excellent. Forty *dinars* a month."

Harry, who was quick, worked it out at six pounds, ten shillings a week. Rose, trying to do the sum, failed (without pencil and paper) and lapsed from the conversation.

Surely, he must be only a kitchen boy for that wage, Harry thought.

"In England, would a good chef have as much?" asked Habib complacently.

Harry was torn between loyalty to his country's system, and the wish not to hurt.

"Perhaps even a little more," he said with a vague air. "I know very little about that business."

"It is a good business," Habib said simply. "Not as

good as yours, I think," he added, glancing at Harry's gold watch, as he had often glanced at it before. Yet, he thought, Rose had nothing grand about *her*—no ear-rings or bracelets, simply a thin plain wedding-ring. Fatma had more. Even his little girls had ear-rings. But wealth—great wealth—seemed indicated all the same. For instance, the Leica camera, the hired car, the hotel. Rose had perhaps been the lucky one, coming to Harry with a small dowry, no paraphernalia, and so thin, too, and with little brown spots—*rousseurs*—all over her face and arms. Beautiful eyes, though, that would look fine *just* seen above the fold of a *haïk*: in the bare face, they looked meaningless.

He toyed with the idea of westernising Fatma, even of bringing her to the café, dressed *à la* Madame Bourguiba, modern, the new Tunisian woman. But it would not do. Who would look after the little girls? It would be expensive. What would his mother say? Reputations would be lost, and difficulties would arise, and Fatma might get ideas into her head.

"Shall we drive you home to the country?" Harry asked, feeling tired—from the wind, and then the sun, and then the beer.

Habib made his pouting, secretive face, and explained in his soft voice that he had to meet a friend later. "I will walk back to the hotel with you while I wait," he said.

They set off down the dark street, stepping carefully over the uneven ground. Trenches being dug for drains were a trap.

Near the hotel was another open, rubbly place.

"Wasn't this, when we came before, a cemetery?" Rose asked.

Habib shivered. "They moved the graves because of the new road," he explained. "But I am still afraid when I walk this way alone at night. One lady," he said, edging closer, more confidentially, towards Harry, "one lady in the town died in child-birth. The next day they went to bury her, and as they were putting her in the ground, she sat up."

"Oh, dear," Rose said. "I don't like that." It was an old horror with her. "Do you have . . ." She sought the word—"*les cercueils?*"

"No." He hesitated, then he stroked his hands over his clothes—the old brown coat—and shuddered.

"Tomorrow," he said, with a change of voice. "I shall be at the café at nine-thirty."

He disappeared, racing back past the place where the cemetery had been, alone, without Harry to protect him from the dead.

The hotel lounge was empty. The Germans had gone to bed early to be in readiness for the sunbathing arrangements of the morrow.

"What a funny holiday," Rose said, when they were in bed. "All alone, except for an Arab chef."

"If he is," Harry said.

"Will he become a bore, a tie?"

"Can't hurt feelings. He's a sensitive fellow. Does no harm to us to spend an hour or two with him."

This was so much what Rose thought that she did not answer. Habib seemed different, away from his café and his comrades. Unshared, she could see him becoming a burden.

"I am longing to see inside an Arab house," she said, "and to meet Fatma and the two little girls."

Now, they were not thinking along the same lines, for Harry had doubts he did not, for her sake, like to voice.

The pattern of their days was pleasant. The weather, though fitful, improved a little, and they drove out to bathing places and stayed the day there, alone, with a picnic lunch of bread and cheese and dates and wine. But the sun was never as hot or the sea as warm to swim in as it had been four years ago and always the wind blew steadily.

In the evenings, after dinner, they met Habib briefly at the café. Apart from him, they rarely spoke to anyone. They were running through the books they had brought.

The wind both chopped and changed, and if there were any shelter to be found, the Germans were there first, with their possessions spread about the terrace. Every morning at about seven, Rose and Harry were wakened by the two men talking outside the window, as they made sure of the *chaises-longues* for the day. There were just enough for their party, and just enough sheltering wall to the terrace. To sit on the sand was impossible. The top layer of it was always shifting in the wind.

One morning, Harry woke up at half-past six to see Rose, in her swimming suit, climbing over the balcony and jumping on to the terrace a foot or two below. She lay down on one *chaise-longue*, and put a book and a towel on the other, and waited for the consternation on the Germans' faces.

The wind had veered round in the night, and the sea beyond the shore road had white caps far out. It looked

most un-Mediterranean. More like the North Sea, Rose
thought. The sun shone, but every minute or so was
obscured by huge, fast-scudding clouds. It will get
warmer later on, Rose thought; but a drop of rain fell on
her bare ankle, then another on her forehead. Just before
the storm broke, she scrambled back over the balcony and
into the bedroom where Harry was warm in bed, and
laughing.

That morning the Germans did not arrive on the terrace.
And once more, Rose had to postpone taking Habib's
photograph.

The rain stopped, and puddles reflected a cold, blue
sky. Rose and Harry, each hiding depression from the
other, went for a walk round the town. The contents of
the shop windows they now knew by heart.

Habib was in the café, sitting just inside the doorway.
For something to do, they joined him and ordered coffee
they did not want. They listened—without any more
amusement—to his tales of grandeur; his fine house and
his fine cooking.

"*Steak au poivre*," he said at random. "What about
that?"

"Not my favourite thing," Harry said, in a grumpy
voice.

Outside the door, on the pavement, the metal chairs
dripped steadily.

"*Soufflé Grand Marnier*," suggested Habib, as if he were
tempting Harry to eat, and Harry said, "I'm not really
hungry."

"As you do not like French cooking, when you come
to my house, we shall eat Tunisian."

"We *do* like French food," Rose said hastily.

He put his lips together in a funny little smile, like a self-conscious child's. Seeing a beggar approaching, he began to rummage in his old purse, and Harry was surprised to see him drop a coin into the outstretched hand. Rather shamefacedly, he did the same. He had thought that only foreigners on their first day out gave alms, and also believed in the English principle that begging should be discouraged.

Habib was in the middle of describing his bedroom at home. Fatma had a dressing-table, he said, with pleated pink silk under a plate-glass top, and bulrushes painted on the mirror. He went into every detail.

"There is one just like that in the carpenter's shop, down the road," Rose said.

He shrugged his shoulders.

"Isn't tomorrow your day off?" she asked, thinking of the excursion into the country to meet Fatma and the children.

"It has been postponed," he said, in an off hand way. "Important guests are arriving at the hotel. I have a special dinner to create. *Asperges, coq au vin . . .*"

Crêpes flambées, thought Harry

"*Crêpes flambées,*" said Habib.

"When's this weather going to improve?" Harry asked sternly. "When shall we have the sun we came for?"

"This afternoon, perhaps: tomorrow, certainly."

"Well, I hope so, I'm sure." Harry was unfairly sharp. It was not Habib's fault that it was cold.

However, he seemed to take the blame for it. He looked put out, then he said, "In England, it is always raining.

Here such weather is exceptional. Such a March has never been known."

When he had left them to go off to his work, they went for a stroll along the shore, walking with their heads bent against the wind. If they could not swim and lie in the sun, there was very little else for them to do.

"Give it another day, and then go home," Harry suggested glumly.

At the edge of the sea, women were doing their washing. There was a rhythmical, slapping sound, as they beat sad old garments into the sandy water.

"We might try Hammamet," Rose said. "It should be more sheltered there." She hated the idea of giving in, of declaring defeat. It was always she who held on longest, hoping to turn their luck, or salvage something. She found it tiring, trying to jolly Harry along at the same time, deluding herself and him, seizing what brightness there was. He was all for cutting losses and clearing out.

It was nearly Independence Day, and some men were putting up triangular red flags in the square. The little flags whipped back and forth against the watery, blue sky.

Harry remembered that Habib had great plans for them for Independence Day. There was to be a procession, and a festival of Tunisian folk music in the cinema. His plans Harry found rather daunting.

A large picture of the President was being hoisted up in the Square.

"Let's go to Habib's hotel for lunch," Harry said, "and sample *la haute cuisine*."

This hotel was also full of people writing postcards.

Rose wondered what they put on them—hopeful messages or lying ones, or cries of despair? On her own cards, she left out mention of the weather. Her friends could assume that it was good—or not, as they chose. The truth would be seen when they arrived home early, pale as all their neighbours, defeated.

They sat on stools at the hotel bar, and Rose stared in front of her, counting bottles, and reading their labels. Her bright conversational openings had at last dried up. She had said all she had to to Harry.

"We have come to try some of Habib's good cooking," Harry said to the barman, who carefully polished a glass, and put it back on a shelf. He appeared not to have understood what was said, and was far too languid to enquire further.

In the dining-room, Rose and Harry looked about them, wondering in what region Habib was practising his new art.

There was an *hors d'œuvre* of tunny fish and raw onion; then some veal, rather tough.

"*Crème caramel*," suggested the waiter, when the veal was finished. *Crème caramel* pursued them—or rather was waiting for them—on all their travels.

"*Crêpes flambées*," suggested Harry.

The waiter shook his head sadly, but the sadness seemed to arise less from the lack of *crêpes* than from Harry's fanciful idea.

"Oh, God, I've let you down again," Harry said, while Rose was eating some dates. "I'm not speaking to God. No! I'm speaking to you. The whole damn holiday's been a fiasco."

"You take too much upon you," she said reprovingly. "You think you can organise everything."

"Well, so I do," he said sullenly. "And in England, so I can."

"Right!" she said decisively. "We'll go to Tunis in the morning, and get a flight home as soon as we can."

She felt some relief at not having to hold on any longer.

"We'll tell Habib tonight."

"No visiting Fatma. No Independence Day procession. No photograph of Habib."

"No picture of Madame Bourguiba, either."

"We won't bother with Hammamet."

"All those dripping orange trees."

"All the same," she said. "This country I love. I was so happy here."

That evening, in the ice-cold café, they told Habib, and he stared down at the table, deeply offended.

"I am sorry we shan't be able to go out to your house in the country," Harry said.

"It is very fine," Habib murmured.

"Today we had lunch at your hotel," Harry said. "Most enjoyable."

"Very nice," Rose said eagerly.

His lips curved upwards very slightly.

"You did not ask for *crêpes flambées*," he said, after a pause.

"They were not on the menu," Harry said cautiously. "Unless we made a mistake."

"You should have commanded. I can arrange anything. If I had known you were coming . . ."

"May we drive you home to the country tonight?" Harry asked.

Habib had never allowed this. He always had some mysterious friend to meet later.

"Tonight, I shall not go to my home. I must be very early at the hotel tomorrow to arrange a banquet for important foreign visitors. In fact, I think I shall now say '*au revoir*' and go to bed early in readiness."

He had tears in his eyes.

"Then where will you stay," asked Harry, and Rose thought that she would not have asked this.

"I have many friends. I shall stay in the *medina*—a very poor little place, but for one night, what does it matter?"

"Well, let us drive you there, at least."

He blinked away his tears and put his head on one side. "As you wish," he said.

In the car, he was silent. Once, he sighed and said what a *dommage* it all was.

"Won't Fatma miss you—out in the country, all on her own?" Harry asked.

"She is accustomed . . . it is one of the hazards of my profession."

They drove into the *medina*, down the widest street, and the only one a car could manage, and Habib leaned over to shake hands with Rose, who was sitting in the back. Then, more emotionally, he put his hand on Harry's shoulder.

"Until our next meeting," he said. "If you would slow down here. My friend's house is nearby."

Rose thought, we shall never meet again.

Harry stopped the car, but not the engine, and with silent dignity Habib clambered out.

The street was empty, and there were stretches of darkness between wall lamps and open doorways.

Habib stood by the car for a second, with his hand lifted. Then he turned away. He was a brief shadow, and then had vanished, as if into the walls of the *medina*.

The first Virago Modern Classic was published in London in 1978, launching a list dedicated to the celebration of women writers and to the rediscovery and reprinting of their works. While the series is called "Modern Classics," it is not true that these works of fiction are universally and equally considered "great," although that is often the case. Published with new critical and biographical introductions, books appear in the series for different reasons: sometimes for their importance in literary history; sometimes because they illuminate particular aspects of women's lives, both personal and public. They may be classics of comedy or storytelling; their interest can be historical, feminist, political, or literary. In any case, in their variety and richness they promise to confuse forever the question of what women's fiction is about, while at the same time affirming a true female tradition in literature.

Initially, the Virago Modern Classics concentrated on English novels and short stories published in the early decades of the century. As the series has grown, it has broadened to include works of fiction from different centuries and from different countries, cultures, and literary traditions; there are books written by black women, by Catholic and Jewish women, by women of almost every English-speaking country, and there are several relevant novels by men.

Nearly 200 Virago Modern Classics will have been published in England by the end of 1985. During that same year, Penguin Books began to publish Virago Modern Classics in the United States, with the expectation of having some forty titles from the series available by the end of 1986. Some of the earlier books in the series were published in the United States by The Dial Press.